LOVE UNDER CONSTRUCTION

PENNY ZELLER

*To my mom, Cindee, the inspiration behind the character Cynthia
Brady. Thank you for being the best mom a girl could have.
I love you.*

I can do all things through Him who strengthens me.
Philippians 4:13

ears pricked Irelynn Brady's eyes. "Please help me," she whispered. Not her first prayer for this situation, and likely far from being her last.

Because God's help was the only way she had any hope of handling the insurmountable task set before her.

Irelynn gripped the steering wheel and glanced in the rearview mirror. The children in the back seat had fallen asleep, exhausted from their hectic day. Their precious round faces weren't the only thing that reminded her she must succeed.

It was also the promise she'd made to their mother, Nicole.

Raindrops splattered on the windshield, and Irelynn flipped on the switch for the windshield wipers. If only the noise of the wipers, combined with the pattering rain, could drown out the emotions that warred within her.

The death of her best friend.

Suddenly becoming a single mom to twin three-year-olds.

A house too small for the unanticipated addition to her family.

And that pesky nemesis, Quinton Gregory, thrown into the mix for good measure.

A woman's voice on the radio interrupted her thoughts. "The

scripture verse of the day is from Philippians 4:13. '*I can do all things through Him who strengthens me.*'"

The comfort from God's Word seeped deep into her heart, and she shoved aside a momentary sliver of apprehension at the stack of burdens that had landed in her lap. The past days had been challenging and turbulent and had left Irelynn wondering how she'd ever succeed at the new role in her life. But succeed, she must.

For the young innocent lives now in her care depended on it.

Moments later, Irelynn inhaled the scent of rain as she hoisted the children, one at a time, into the house. She tucked in one, then the other, into their toddler beds that she'd moved from Nicole's house and into her own room. The two remained sleeping, although Max stirred and mumbled "Mama" in his sleep.

Irelynn's heart broke. She had no right to complain when these children had lost so much.

She was about to dash to her car to retrieve her purse and the kids' overnight bags when her phone rang. She recognized the number and grabbed it before the ring tone could awaken the twins.

"Hello?"

"Irelynn?"

"Hi, Jamie."

"Do you have a minute?"

"Sure." Irelynn stepped back onto the porch and watched the torrential downpour. Better to be out here in the weather underneath the protective porch roof than inside fearing she'd awaken the twins.

"As you know, business has slowed as of late."

Irelynn held her breath and braced herself for Jamie's next comment.

"As such," her boss continued, "I'll have to cut your hours to part-time for the foreseeable future. Dan is doing some marketing in the hopes of drumming up business, but it'll probably be a while before we see the fruits of his labor."

Irelynn swallowed hard. She needed this job, especially now that she was partially responsible for Mia and Max.

"Irelynn, are you still there?"

She took a deep breath. "I'm still here."

"Good. Look. I know this comes at a bad time, but we are hopeful it's only temporary. I would completely understand if you needed to find a different job with more hours."

"Thank you, I appreciate that." What else could she say? Yes, she needed a job with more hours. A new mortgage and family didn't afford her many options when it came to finances.

The conversation ended, and Irelynn clicked off. Could things get any worse?

Tears flowed freely then, and Irelynn lifted another prayer heavenward. How could she support the twins on her now meager income? She couldn't...wouldn't let Nicole down.

Doing her best to shove the concerning thoughts aside, Irelynn dodged out to the car for the items she'd sought to retrieve before the phone rang. The sound of a vehicle driving down the road captured her attention. Squinting, she realized it was just who she did not want to see.

I have to see him twice in one day?

The newer model pickup truck pulled into her driveway behind her car, and Mr. Arrogance himself stepped out of the truck and into the rain. Irelynn took cover on the porch. What could the man possibly want?

Then her eyes settled on something held loosely in his grasp. Mia's baby doll.

Quinton Gregory stepped onto the porch and shook the rain from his blond hair. "Mia forgot this."

Irelynn wrapped her arms around herself in an attempt to warm herself from the cold breeze. "They're sleeping, so I'll give it to her."

He looked as though he didn't believe her. "All right."

Quinton seemed to see right through her. Could he tell that she'd been crying? More like sobbing. She absolutely, positively, would not let him know that there had been times in the past few days when she'd felt as though she was on the brink of failure.

"Thank you," Irelynn said, taking the doll from him.

Quinton nodded, but said nothing. Instead, he sprinted back to his truck through the downpour of rain without so much as a backward glance in her direction.

What were the odds that the man who had stood her up on their first and only date would be the one with whom she'd have to share custody of two children?

QUINTON SQUINTED through the rain as he backed out of Irelynn's driveway and headed back to his apartment.

This entire trip across town could be considered a waste of time.

But it wasn't.

Fifteen minutes after he'd loaded the children into Irelynn's car, Quinton had discovered Mia's favorite doll, whom she'd named Baby, left behind on the couch.

When Mia realized she didn't have her prized possession, she'd be crushed. That thought had crushed *him*. So, without hesitation, Quinton had grabbed the doll, locked up his one-bedroom apartment, and raced to his truck.

Not that he'd wanted to see Irelynn Brady, especially since she was so unfriendly and standoffish. And he certainly didn't expect to carry on a conversation.

Pulling into the parking lot of his apartment complex several minutes later, Quinton made a beeline up two sets of stairs and unlocked the door of his apartment.

The still quiet contrasted the laughter and energetic noises of two toddlers from mere hours ago.

He already missed them.

Might as well do something to keep his mind occupied. He was way too hyped up to call it a day.

Quinton finished hauling in the second dresser to his room—or rather the twins' room. Everything had changed since his sister passed away, leaving him with joint custody of his niece and nephew. He arched his shoulders back in an effort to stretch out his muscles after lifting the furniture.

But the strain in his back and shoulders wasn't only from hauling and rearranging furniture.

Far from it.

Losing his sister to cancer had taken a toll on him. He and Nicole had been close their entire lives and even more so since they'd lost their parents. They had clung to each other, knowing it was only them and their Gram left. Grief overwhelmed him. Why had God taken her so soon?

Now Mia and Max were orphans at three-years-old. First their dad, Tom, while deployed in Afghanistan, and now their mom.

Tom. Quinton took a deep breath. Tom should still be here. He should be the one raising his children after the loss of their mom.

If only you'd kept him safe like you promised Nicole you would. The words of guilt nipped at Quinton's conscience.

If Quinton failed to keep a grown man safe in enemy territory, how could he manage to successfully care for two children?

Combine the death of his sister, his new status as a single dad, the guilt of not saving Tom, the stress of reviving the family construction business, and dealing with that uppity and irresponsible Irelynn Brady...it was enough to slam him into stress overload.

Irelynn Brady. The woman who shared custody with him. Apparently, Nicole had seen something in the best friend she had acquired while Quinton was deployed to allow the woman to help raise her children.

While it appeared Irelynn genuinely cared about Nicole and the twins, Quinton hadn't seen anything that really impressed him enough to agree with Nicole's decision about something of this magnitude. Hadn't seen it at the church. At the funeral, or the very first time he'd met the woman at Nicole's bedside. Or the day she stood him up for the "date" Nicole had arranged. No call, no text, no explanation.

Just a "no show."

Anyone irresponsible enough to miss a date set up by their dying best friend didn't strike him as someone who could be responsible enough to help care for two of the most important people in Quinton's life.

CHAPTER 2

Irelynn stared at her somewhat-of-a-nemesis. He stared right back. As if they were both involved in some type of showdown in the old Wild West.

Tall, handsome, blond, athletic...and arrogant.

Would he apologize for standing her up? Good thing Nicole hadn't known. She would have had his hide.

Taking a deep breath, Irelynn stepped to the side, and with barely a nod in her direction, Quinton stepped into the foyer.

"Uncle Quinton!" Two three-year-olds ran to their uncle's open arms. He scooped up Mia and Max and captured them in a giant bear hug.

"How are my two favorite kids?" Quinton asked.

Mia giggled and planted a kiss on the stubble on Quinton's chin.

Not that Irelynn noticed whether or not there was stubble on his chin.

Max snuggled into Quinton's chest, and Quinton placed a kiss on each of their foreheads. "How about I give you both a ride to where your new rooms will be?"

Irelynn watched, feeling much more like a spectator viewing a family movie than the owner of her home.

"Where's the room?" Quinton asked, his gaze connecting with hers for but a brief moment.

"I'll show you."

As if they had done this a million times, the twins, one on each bicep, clasped their fingers around his arms. Quinton carried them, as they giggled the entire way.

Irelynn unlocked the door at the end of the hall and opened it to a dusty unfinished addition. She shivered as a cool draft escaped the room. "I'm not sure what the previous owners planned for this area. It's as if they started the project, but never finished it." Surely Quinton Gregory of Gregory Home Building and Remodeling could turn the dreary and dank add-on into two separate rooms for the children now under Irelynn's care.

After all, his business came highly recommended.

Even if Irelynn herself would not have chosen him.

She stepped aside and allowed Quinton to peer into the room. "It'll have to be divided into two rooms," he said.

Why had Nicole insisted her brother be the one to renovate? Surely the prospect of having to share custody of the twins after Nicole's passing was enough. Irelynn didn't need Quinton's help with the renovation too. But Nicole had insisted that he undertake the job and only charge Irelynn for the materials.

Irelynn should feel grateful. Labor would cost her a fortune if she had gone with another company. A fortune she did not have, especially with the dismal news concerning her job. Free labor aside, however, there was something about Quinton that irritated her. And not just his lack of respect in failing to arrive at the restaurant where he promised he'd meet Irelynn. His being in her presence even more than necessary was not going to help matters. Otherwise, Irelynn may have been able to forget the whole "date" ordeal.

Quinton kneeled and spoke softly to the children. "You two go play for a few minutes while I look at your new room."

"Can't we go in there with you?" Mia asked, always the voice for the two.

"No, honey, it's not safe," Irelynn answered, planting a kiss on the tops of each of their heads. "Why don't you go finish the pictures you were coloring so you can show them to Uncle Quinton after he looks at the room?"

The two scampered off, and Irelynn stepped into the gloomy room. "There are no lights, only what comes through the windows. I'm not even sure there's electricity in here."

Quinton sauntered around the room, hands in the pockets of his jeans. "It will take a lot of work to divide the room and finish it so it's safe. I'm surprised it even passed inspection when you bought the house." He looked at her. Was that judgment in his eyes?

Irelynn quirked an eyebrow. Why did she feel the need to defend herself? "I was thankful to have found this house. This room being the exception, the rest of the place was in immaculate condition and was offered at a very fair price. Surely you understand as a homeowner that there can be issues with just about any house purchased." Mom would have declared the tone of her voice as saucy for sure.

"I don't own my own home, I rent an apartment."

"Oh. Then you wouldn't know about home ownership." That came out far snarkier than she had intended.

Quinton shrugged and continued his perusal. "Have you had this room tested for mold?"

"What makes you think there's mold?"

"The smell? Could be the windows leaked moisture at some point."

Irelynn took a whiff of the room. It did smell musty, and had from the moment she had opened the door on that first day when taking a tour of the home.

"The kids need to live in a mold-free home. Nicole had asthma, so one or both of them could have inherited it."

"Yes, and in no way would I allow them to live in a home full of mold."

"Good. Then you should have it tested."

Why was the man so infuriating?

Anyone else mentioning it, and Irelynn wouldn't have given it a second thought. But since it was Quinton...

And to think that Nicole had mentioned that she thought Irelynn and Quinton should date each other—and then proceeded to urge them to go on a blind date of sorts. *"My brother really is a terrific guy. You just need to give him a chance. Besides, I think you two would make a great pair."*

Uh huh. And Irelynn was the Queen of England. Having any interest at all in Quinton Gregory was so not going to happen.

Ever.

~

QUINTON HADN'T EXPECTED the renovation to be so extensive when Nicole made him promise to undertake the labor portion of the job. *"She'll need somewhere for the children. Unfortunately, her home only has one room. When she bought the house, she didn't anticipate..."*

Nicole's words had drifted, and Quinton had done his best to comfort his sister that he would do all he could to ensure that the addition would be remodeled and made suitable for the twins.

He recalled her thin, fragile frame in those last days, and how he had begged the Lord to heal her. No one could have anticipated the cancer that abruptly overtook Nicole's body at the age of 25. Quinton swallowed hard. Would the pain of losing her ever get any easier?

But Quinton would have promised Nicole just about anything. Especially since Nicole, Gram, and the twins were the last family he had left. Still, why hadn't his sister given him full custody of Mia and Max? It would have made life so much easier, even if being a single dad was so far out of his realm, he at times couldn't conceive it. Nicole's gentle voice echoed through his mind. *"You really should give Irelynn a chance. She's the sweetest person you ever met. So caring and kind. I think you two would make a great pair."*

Quinton hadn't wanted to hurt Nicole's feelings, especially in her weakened state, but there was no way he'd ever take any interest in Irelynn Brady, and that was before she decided to stand him up for their so-called date.

While he had been away in the military for four years, Nicole had become best friends with the woman who had recently moved to their hometown of Chokecherry Heights. Why they had become friends, Quinton couldn't fathom.

Sure. Irelynn was pretty. Beautiful even. If one went by looks only. But based on Quinton's limited time of knowing her, he found the woman to be standoffish and snobby. Plus, the woman's rudeness over the date without so much as an apology was just plain... Yes, something about her just got to him.

And not in a good way.

"This place definitely needs help," he muttered, continuing his perusal of the room. "I wonder if it's even on a foundation."

Irelynn rolled her eyes at him. "I know for a fact this house is on a foundation. Excuse me a moment. I need to check on the twins." Without waiting for his answer, she left the room. He followed her into the living room where Mia and Max were sprawled on the living room floor coloring pictures.

It was obvious when she spun about abruptly and collided with him that she hadn't anticipated him following her. "Oops. Excuse me." Her face resembled a color akin to a ripe strawberry, and Quinton did his best to hide his amusement.

Irelynn was apparently doing her best to regain her composure when she added in a squeaky voice, "Where do you propose we start?"

"The first thing we need to do is open a charge account for you at Nathanson's."

She appeared mortified. "A charge account?"

Did the woman pay for everything with cash? Must be nice. "Yes. A charge account. That way, I can get whatever I need as far as building supplies go."

Her green eyes widened. Not that he noticed she had green eyes. "Oh."

"Trust me. I'll only buy the materials to fix the room. No power tools, unless absolutely necessary." Could she tell he was making an attempt to lighten the mood? The newest and sleekest power tools were his weakness, not that he would ever purchase them on a client's account. Honesty was of utmost importance to him.

"Look, why don't we go to Nathanson's right now and open the account? That way I can get started this week on the rooms." The sooner he finished this project, the better. No sense in having to be around her more than necessary. It was enough to retrieve the kids when it was his turn to take care of them and deliver them when it was again her turn.

Irelynn appeared hesitant, and he added, "Feel free to open an account on your own. I just thought while we were there, we could look at some flooring and maybe some paint colors."

Her eyes darted around, and it reminded Quinton of those suspicious people on the cop shows he and Nicole watched when they were younger. Finally, she answered. "Sure. Do you know how long it will take to remodel the room?"

Quinton blew out a long breath of air. Things had been busy lately with two new houses going up in the new Waterbury Acres Subdivision and the remodel project on Fourth Street. Not that he was complaining. The Lord had blessed him richly with enough business to hire three full-time workers. But Quinton had to make Irelynn's project a priority.

For Mia and Max.

And for Nicole.

"I'm not sure. Once I get started, I'll have a better idea. Shouldn't take too long."

Unless more needed to be done than Quinton first antici-pated, which was entirely possible, given the condition of the room.

"Good. I was hoping it would be quick."

They stared at each other for what seemed like several awkward moments. What was it about this odd woman? At least he only had to deal with her until Mia and Max were 18. Fifteen long years.

The things he did for his sister.

CHAPTER 3

*I*f there was one word to describe the fact that she, Irelynn Brady, would be taking a home improvement jaunt with Quinton Gregory, it would be *awkward*.

As she opened the door of Quinton's silver pickup truck and placed Max in the backseat on the passenger's side, Irelynn caught a glimpse of Mrs. Caruthers next door. Sure enough, the cantankerous older woman was writing furiously in her hand-held notebook. Every so often, she would glance up, adjust her dark-rimmed glasses, scrutinize her surroundings, and then write again.

"Who is that woman?" Quinton asked, as he buckled Mia into her seat.

"Mrs. Caruthers. She's harmless, but she's always taking notes."

Quinton nodded. "I noticed that when I drove up to your house. She had stepped out on her porch and was taking notes then too. What's her deal, anyway?"

Irelynn shrugged, amazed that she and Quinton were actually carrying on somewhat of a decent conversation. How much should she say? Irelynn didn't want Quinton thinking his niece and nephew had dangerous or shady neighbors. "I'm not sure. I haven't formally met her yet." She dared another glance in the woman's direction. This time, Mrs. Caruthers was squinting, her head, topped with gray spikey hair, tilted to one side as she appeared to analyze her victims. Irelynn smiled, making a mental note to have the kids help her bake cookies to take to Mrs. Caruthers. Perhaps she would find a friend in the eccentric elderly woman.

Friendship. When Nicole died, Irelynn lost a lot more than a best friend. She'd lost the sister she'd always wanted, but never had.

Would the pain of losing Nicole ever get easier?

With the exception of Mia asking a few questions, the drive to Nathanson's was quiet. Quinton waved at nearly everyone they passed. Did the man know the entire population of Chokecherry Heights? When Irelynn had moved here with her mom just over three years ago, they were both ready for small-town living. But Irelynn still hadn't forged many close friendships. 'Twas the case for an introvert, she supposed. She recalled that Nicole said she had grown up in Chokecherry Heights. What would it be like to reside in the same town you'd been born in, graduated from high school in, and raised your family?

Nathanson's, the only home improvement store in town, was as usual, filled with customers. Max squealed when he saw the special shopping carts with steering wheels. "Can we wide in dat?" he begged, pointing with a stubby finger.

Mia appeared less excited. "Can Baby come?" she pleaded, gripping her dolly close by her side.

"Yes, you can ride in the special car cart, and yes, Mia, Baby can come."

At least the twins seemed to be adjusting somewhat after their mom's passing.

Irelynn caught a sideways glimpse of Quinton pushing the children in the cart. They appeared as though they were some family on their way to purchase new flooring or perhaps some materials for a weekend project. A part of her wistfully wondered what it would have been like to have a dad in her life to partake in such projects.

"We'll go to the front desk first so we can set up your charge account," Quinton said.

Was the man always this bossy?

"How are you today, Quinton?" the man behind the counter asked and leaned forward.

"Doing good, Frank. We're here to set up a charge account for Irelynn. I'll be doing some remodeling on a room in her house."

"Well, you've hired the right man for the job," said Frank, smiling at Irelynn.

Irelynn wasn't so sure. But with free labor, that had to count for something, right? Frank handed her an application. "What amount are you looking at for the charge limit?"

Their voices chimed in at the same time, although with vastly different amounts.

"$500?"

"How about between $5,000-$7,000?"

Had Irelynn just heard an amount in the *thousands*? She felt her jaw drop, and she discreetly checked her heart rate on her fitness tracker. Sure enough, her pulse had significantly quickened.

"Well, I can see we're a bit different on our guestimates," chuckled Frank.

Of course, Frank didn't realize this was nothing to make light of. It could be years before Irelynn would be able to pay back Nathanson's. Maybe even centuries with her job now being part-time. Perhaps she should just resign to the fact that Mia and Max would be "camping out" in her meager room until they were tweens.

Quinton faced her. "Irelynn, it will take about $5,000-$7,000 to finish those two rooms."

"But I thought you had agreed to do the labor for free."

"That is with free labor."

Frank cleared his throat. "I'll give you two some time to sort this out while I help the next customer. I'll be right back."

Irelynn glanced at the twins. They needed their own rooms, and she needed to prove she could raise them. If she gave even a hint that she was unable to financially provide for them, she wouldn't be able to keep her promise to her dear friend. She needed to be able to secure more hours with her current job and maybe even find a second job.

"It might not cost that much. I try to do things economically, but you also don't want to use the cheapest products that aren't going to last," Quinton said.

Irelynn rolled her eyes. The guy was likely a pro at persuasion. How often had he quipped this very same line to all of his customers? "All right," she muttered.

"Now that we've gotten that taken care of..." Quinton strutted back to the counter, as if he'd just won an important race. Was there not an ounce of uncockiness in the man's body?

Uncockiness is not a word, Irelynn. Crotchety old Mrs. Smith's voice from ninth grade English echoed around in Irelynn's mind.

"I just need you to complete the top portion and sign here." Frank pointed a beefy finger at the bottom of the application.

Irelynn willed her hands not to shake as she perused the short, but serious form. Taking in a deep breath, she signed her name. Her financial future suddenly became even gloomier. Peanut butter and jelly sandwiches for every meal for the next 40 years wasn't so bad, was it?

"All right then. You're all set." Frank tossed a grin Irelynn's way. "Good luck on the remodeling project."

"Thanks." Irelynn tried to ignore the fact that her voice came out sounding nasally and unlike her own. Thankfully, she didn't believe in luck. But she did believe in miracles. And the Giver of those miracles.

Quinton suggested they first look at the flooring options. "It'll be a while before we need it, but it's always worthwhile to see what options there are. You'll also need to figure out what color of paint you'd like for each room."

Irelynn thought she might be in shock. It was all so overwhelming, and all she could hear was the ching-chinging of money in her mind, as he pointed out each "necessity."

Quinton took off at an energetic clip, veering the car cart through the aisles, much to the children's delight. "Race car number 77 speeds past the competition," he announced, sounding like a commentator.

Thankful she had buckled the kids into their shopping cart seats, Irelynn increased her pace as well. Mia and Max giggled and made car sounds and spun the steering wheel. "Go faster," Mia squealed as she clapped her hands.

Quinton gave commentary the entire way to the flooring area, pretending that displays of products were other cars. "And then they pass a beat-up old truck."

"A beat-up tuck," giggled Max.

If Irelynn's dad had stuck around, would he have played creative games like this with shopping carts when he took Irelynn shopping with him?

She swallowed the thought. Why think about things to which she'd never know the answer?

Minutes later, the twins were disappointed when Quinton stopped at the flooring samples. "Laminate is the way to go these days," he said, changing gears from pretending to be a professional race car driver back to Quinton of Gregory Home Building and Remodeling.

Before Irelynn could answer, a voice boomed out of nowhere. "Quinton, my man!" A jolly-faced young man slugged Quinton in the shoulder, then did some sort of strange handshake, followed by a fist bump. "I heard you got back from Afghanistan. How have you been?"

"Doing good, Carlos." Quinton returned the handshake, followed by a few more fist bumps.

Carlos took a step back. "Say, man, when did you get married and have a family? Has it been that long since we last saw each other?"

Irelynn stared in shock. This man thought...

Quinton laughed. "These are my niece and nephew, Mia and Max. Nicole's kids."

"I heard about her. Sorry about her passing."

Quinton nodded, but Irelynn could see the emotion just beneath the surface.

"And this is your beautiful wife?"

Irelynn noticed that Quinton didn't laugh this time. Rather, he looked perturbed at Carlos's suggestion. The feeling was mutual. "Uh, no. This is Irelynn Brady."

"Friends?"

"I'm doing a remodel of a room in her house." Irelynn didn't blame Quinton for not saying they were friends. They were barely acquaintances. More like nemeses. Especially since he was a "date-dodger". She inwardly chuckled at her made-up description of him.

Carlos nodded. "Gotcha. And here I was thinking you were already married with a family. Do you remember Chandra?"

"Yes."

Carlos leaned toward Quinton as if to share an important secret. "She and I are getting married."

"Is she feeling okay?" Quinton asked, obviously ribbing his friend.

"Very funny. I'd love it if you would come to the wedding. I'll see that you get an invitation." Carlos paused. "Oh, and you too, Irelynn, you should come too. That way Quinton doesn't have to try to find a date, which could be a challenge for him."

"Oh, I wouldn't want to impose." And she could just imagine how hard it would be for Quinton to find a date. After all, what woman wanted to spend time with someone who couldn't even bother showing up for a date?

"Not an imposition at all. It'd be awesome to have you come as Quinton's date."

That was the last thing that Irelynn wanted to do, but she didn't want to be unkind to Carlos. He seemed like a nice fellow and super excited about his upcoming wedding.

"What do you say, Quinton?" Carlos prodded.

Quinton shrugged.

"Sounds like a plan then." Carlos turned to Irelynn. "Quinton and I ran track together back in the day. This guy could really run then before he got all old and stodgy."

"Hey, I still run," countered Quinton. "And old and stodgy? Look who's talking." He playfully pointed at Carlos's ample gut.

Irelynn watched as the two continued to joke. Did she really want to go with Quinton to Carlos's wedding? *The answer to that question is an astounding "no!"*

She could only hope that by the time the wedding date rolled around, Quinton would forget all about Carlos inviting her.

Then horror struck. What if she showed up at Carlos's wedding all by herself because Quinton stood her up again?

QUINTON PUSHED the cart through the rest of the store. Much as he'd like to stay at Nathanson's the remainder of the afternoon, the kids were likely getting hungry, and he had some bids to work on tonight. Besides, it was doubtful Irelynn enjoyed the excursion. Who'd have thought she'd be so ungrateful and uptight about the remodel? He would do his best to complete the job as frugally as possible, as he did with all of his customers, but the price of materials was high these days. And he wanted his niece and nephew to have nice rooms.

Speaking of nice rooms...he needed to do something in the

near future about his own living arrangement. The apartment was hardly big enough for him and the kids. Quinton had his eye on two different houses for sale in Chokecherry Heights in his price range: one over on Fourth Street near a customer's home, and the other just down the street from Irelynn's house. He'd rather build one, but given the circumstances, a larger home was a necessity sooner rather than later.

The pluses of each house thrummed through his mind at a rapid pace. It would be easier to retrieve and drop off the twins per the custody arrangement if he chose the house down the street from Irelynn's home. And it did have running paths nearby for him and a park for the twins, plus close proximity to town for when he became a "soccer dad." Major downside? Having to cross paths with Irelynn more than necessary if he chose to live in her neighborhood. The pluses of the Fourth Street house: not near Irelynn, less remodeling, and a bigger yard for the kids. Downsides? Far from town, inconvenient, more expensive, and not as nice of a neighborhood.

More prayer and seeking advice from Gram were in order before he could make a decision.

His mind reverted to Irelynn. The expression on her face rather amused Quinton when Carlos thought he and Irelynn were married. She had blushed, the same way she had when they'd collided in her house earlier.

Man, what is your deal? Why are you noticing Irelynn's face? The only thing he should be noticing is that at least they were in agreement about one thing: their dislike for each other.

But did he really have to take her to Carlos's wedding as his date? Maybe she would forget all about it when the time came. More likely, she'd not even bother to show. A repeat of the date incident. Carlos would never let Quinton live that down.

He caught a glimpse of Irelynn from the corner of his eye. She was an attractive woman with her brown hair and expressive eyes. But she gave such a snobby air. Did she think he wouldn't be honest in his dealings with his sister's best friend? While he didn't care much for Irelynn, Quinton didn't have a dishonest bone in his body. Dad always said to make sure your word was gold. And Quinton lived by that goal. What he said, he did.

Except for saving Tom's life. The guilt of being unable to save his brother-in-law penetrated Quinton's heart. Hadn't he promised Nicole he would bring her husband safely back from Afghanistan? *Liar.*

He needed to clear his mind. Looking at the varieties of lumber in the lumber department always did that. "Max and I are going to head over to the lumber section. We can meet you back here in a while."

Irelynn cast him a glance like she really didn't care if he went to the lumber department or took a permanent vacation to the North Pole. "Come on, sweetie," she said to Mia, lifting her out of the cart. To him, she added, "Mia and I will be in the appliances area. You can take the cart."

Quinton headed toward the lumber department with Max. The thought thrilled him that it wouldn't be long before he would be teaching Max—and Mia too—all about building materials. They would start with a simple birdhouse, just as Dad had done with him and Nicole. They'd graduate to the point where he would build them a treehouse, an exact duplicate of the one Dad had built all those years ago, and that Nicole had never stopped talking about.

The scent of lumber filled Quinton's nostrils and he inhaled. "Smell that, Max? It's the smell of creativity."

Max gave him a confused look. As they wandered through the aisles of nicely stacked wood, Quinton explained to Max all about the different sizes, types, and grains.

After his brief time of lumber therapy, Quinton pushed Max back toward the appliance department. The sight he saw stopped his heart.

Irelynn had lifted Mia so she could see the top of a two-door oven and was inspecting the knobs and features. Quinton held up a finger to his lips for Max not to say a word, not that the little guy said much anyway, and pushed the cart closer.

"I love these types of stoves, Mia," she was saying, her back to Quinton and Max. She set Mia down and leaned over to open one oven door, then the other. "Wouldn't it be fun to bake cookies in both of these ovens?"

Quinton watched, mesmerized by her. Most women wanted designer clothes or shoes or spa treatments. Irelynn wanted a stove. To bake cookies. With his niece.

"Yes," agreed Mia, likely thinking only of the result of baking, rather than the actual logistics.

"We could make cookies for the entire neighborhood. Chocolate chip and snickerdoodles."

"I like those kinds," declared Mia, her blonde curls bouncing as she bobbed her head.

"Me too."

"And we could make some for me and Max and Uncle Quinton. He likes cookies."

As Irelynn and Mia carried on their conversation about cookies, and as Irelynn marveled over the stove, a peculiar feeling came over Quinton.

And for some strange reason, just for a brief minute, Quinton wished he could buy her that oven. He'd seen the archaic one she had at her house.

But as quickly as the thought entered his mind, he dismissed it.

No way would he let Irelynn Brady get to him.

CHAPTER 4

Mia and Max ran through the door in a flurry, slowing down just long enough to give Irelynn's mother a giant hug before heading to the box of toys in the corner of the room. Irelynn plopped on the recliner and let out a huff of exasperation.

"Sounds serious. I'll put the coffee on," said Mom, as she headed to the kitchen of her humble townhouse.

It was serious, all right. Irelynn wasn't sure she was equipped to raise two unruly toddlers *and* deal with an annoying home renovator.

Mom reappeared a few moments later with two steaming cups of coffee. She handed Irelynn one cup, then sat down in the rocking chair opposite of her daughter. "So...do tell."

Irelynn laughed. Mom had said those exact words whenever there was a "crisis" since Irelynn was in elementary school. "I hope I turn out to be half as good of a mom as you are."

"Motherhood is hard, but you're doing an admirable job of it, Irelynn. Especially since you had two little ones practically dropped in your lap less than a month ago."

Mia and Max looked preoccupied with the new set of toy

jumbo building blocks, and Irelynn lowered her voice and leaned toward her mother. "I want to succeed at this, Mom, I really do. But it's hard. I love them to pieces, but I'm not sure it's the best option to have them split between Quinton and me."

Mom appeared to ponder Irelynn's statement before responding. Irelynn appreciated that about her. She herself didn't have that gift of pondering first, then speaking. Rather, Irelynn was the opposite, much to her own chagrin.

"I take it that Quinton isn't returning to active duty?"

"I don't think so. He seems content running his home-building and remodeling business."

"Nicole had originally planned for you both to care for the children, especially in light of the fact that Quinton might again be deployed, and they would need care while he was away. It seems I remember you telling me she was afraid of something happening to Quinton, as it had her husband."

Irelynn nodded. She remembered the day Nicole received the news that her husband, Tom, had been killed by a roadside bomb. "Yes, and I know Quinton and I were all she had left as far as someone raising the twins since Nicole and Quinton's grandmother is living in an assisted living facility. But, Mom, what if I fail?" She could feel the tears threatening and lowered her voice even more so the children couldn't hear the conversation.

Mom placed a soft hand on Irelynn's wrist. "You won't fail. God doesn't give us an assignment without seeing us through it."

"I know, and I believe that, Mom, but sometimes it feels like it's all too much. And then there's Quinton. He's so annoying. He doesn't seem to think anything about my house is good enough for the twins. He practically demanded I go with him to Nathanson's and open up a charge account. Mom, we both know I don't have that kind of money, especially with Jamie having to cut my hours."

"Did you explain to him your situation?"

Irelynn bit her lip. Never would her pride allow her to inform her "somewhat-of-a-nemesis" of her soon-to-be dire financial situation. If she did, Quinton might decide she wasn't competent enough to care for the children, and Irelynn could never have anything or anyone come in the way of her promise to Nicole. "No. He sarcastically promised that he wouldn't charge any power tools on my account. That was not humorous to me at all. I know it's going to cost a certain amount to remodel that room, but I honestly don't have the funds to make it look like something in a magazine or online. I've seen the houses this guy builds. They're amazing. My house must look like a shack to him."

"In all fairness, he was probably trying to lighten the mood when he said that about the power tools."

Irelynn narrowed her eyes. "Mom, are you siding with the enemy?"

Mom feigned a shocked look. "Never. You have my loyalty—all 100 percent of it. However, from the few times I spoke with Quinton, he seemed very charming."

"Charming to everyone but me."

"This is a tough situation. Perhaps he's feeling the stress of it as well."

Irelynn hadn't given any thought that the overly-confident Quinton Gregory would experience stress, but she supposed it would be true. "It probably is hard for him being a new single dad," she admitted. "Especially with losing his sister. Nicole always mentioned how close they were."

"I wish the two of you could work together on this, at least for the children's sake, and as part of your promise to Nicole. Instead, it seems both of you see each other as the adversary."

"He is the adversary," Irelynn muttered. She took another sip of her coffee.

Mom gave her the "mom look," one that Irelynn feared she would likely inherit. "The adversary?"

"Anyone who stands up a date is an adversary. I can understand if he would have texted or called saying there was a change of plans, or even apologized after the fact…" Irelynn recalled that evening so clearly. Embarrassment had overwhelmed her as she sat at Fernando's Italian Restaurant all alone and downing a week's worth of carbs from the complimentary bread bowl while waiting for Quinton.

"Well, let's just hope he had a valid reason. Have you asked him?"

Mom. Always the optimist.

"No, I haven't asked him." *Shouldn't he volunteer that information?*

"Now, as far as the funds go," said Mom, who in her gracious way changed the subject. "Perhaps you could see if another web design company is hiring. You have an artistic gift, Irelynn." Mom paused. "I am more than happy to watch the kids those two days I'm off work each week so you can take on another part-time job, if necessary. The nice thing about your current job is that you can work from home. I'll be praying they pick up more accounts and you can return to full-time. That would be so much easier than another part-time job."

"Oh, Mom, you do so much for me. What would I do without you?" Irelynn leaned forward and gave Mom a one-armed hug, mindful of the coffee mugs. And truly, what would she do without Mom? The woman had sacrificed everything to raise Irelynn on her own.

Irelynn sat back on the recliner and folded her legs beneath her. "Would you like to hear about the horrific event that happened Monday when we went to Nathanson's when Quinton decided I needed to open a charge account?"

"Horrific event?"

"Oh, it was horrific all right, and I'm not just talking about the high credit limit. Anyway, some friend of Quinton's named Carlos saw us and thought we were married." Irelynn cringed. "Can you imagine?"

Mom laughed. "There are a lot worse people you could be married to, Irelynn."

"Really? Like who?" Irelynn herself laughed then, thankful for a moment of reprieve from the stress of the past month.

"What I think is really funny," said Mom, "is that you two sit in the same row at church, only on opposite ends. Maybe if circumstances were different, you might actually like him."

"Nope, nada, not going to happen. He's only been there twice since he was apparently going to the second service before he realized it was much easier for both of us to go to the first service."

"Not that you're noticing his church attendance schedule," Mom teased.

"If you keep harassing me, Mom, I'll have no choice but to remind you about Mr. Wilson who sits directly behind us at church and seems to have taken an interest in you."

Mom put up her hands in surrender. "All right, truce."

"Memaw, look what I built," said Mia presenting a creation made of toy building blocks to her grandma.

"That's really neat, Mia. Tell me about it."

Mia appeared thoughtful, her upturned nose scrunched and her eyes looking upward. "It's a tree house like Mommy and Uncle Quinton's."

Mom oohed and aahed over Mia's creation and Irelynn wondered how many times Nicole had shared the story about the childhood treehouse with her children. The one Nicole's dad had built special for her and Quinton.

Irelynn had a deep appreciation for Mom. At a time when her mother should be taking it easier, due to health concerns, Mom insisted on doing all she could to help Irelynn and to fill the role of grandma to two orphans.

"The kids are fortunate to have you for a grandma, Mom."

"And they're fortunate to have you too, Irelynn."

Mia traipsed over to Max and the pile of building blocks and started another creation.

"I hope so," Irelynn said, her voice a whisper. "I worry about them. Both have a hard time sleeping, and Max says so few words."

"Perhaps with Mia being the chatterbox of the two, he can be a man of few words, as the saying goes," suggested Mom.

"True. She does say most of the words for them. Maybe I'll give it awhile longer and then have him checked to see if he needs speech lessons. I do worry, though, when they both wake up crying sometimes at night. They miss Nicole so much."

"Yes, and nothing can be harder on little ones than losing their mom."

Irelynn nodded. If only the Lord hadn't taken Nicole so soon.

THAT EVENING, Irelynn finished putting the dishes away. The wall rack, which doubled as a kitchen shelf with important keepsakes on it, beckoned her. On the second shelf, a photo frame she had made during an outing with Nicole at a women's craft event at church, invited her attention. Colorful buttons lined the edges of the frame, and two faces in a photo within its borders stared back at her.

She and Nicole both smiled for the camera, unaware that their time together was short. It had been a memorable evening at the craft event, one that had reminded them both that their crafting skills were sorely lacking. Still, they'd both taken it in stride, even when their button frames resembled something akin to a kindergartener's art project.

Tears stung Irelynn's eyes. She would have done just about anything for her best friend. Even go on a crazy date with Nicole's brother.

Quinton could have at least appeased his sister when Nicole had arranged for them to meet for dinner at a restaurant in town.

But for reasons unknown to Irelynn, he'd let his sister down on something that had meant so much to her.

"It'll be fun," insisted Nicole, her pale face lighting up with her suggestion.

"Nicole..."

Nicole had placed a cold hand on Irelynn's arm. "Just give him a chance. For me. If you don't like him after giving him a chance, you'll be under no obligation."

"You sound like a TV ad," giggled Irelynn.

"Think of it this way," said Nicole. "It'll be like one of those quirky blind dates in the chick flicks we enjoy watching." She paused, as if the conversation drained her.

Irelynn wanted to insist it wasn't a blind date since she and Quinton were acquaintances, and this was far different than watching a chick flick movie marathon, but she refrained. "All right, Nicole. Where should we go?"

"How about Fernando's?" her weak voice was now almost a whisper. "Would 7:00 Friday night work?"

That was only a few days away. "How about next month?" Irelynn asked, attempting to lighten the mood.

Nicole shifted and grimaced from the pain. "This Friday would be better."

A horrible thought struck Irelynn then. Nicole needed the date to be as soon as possible because she didn't have much time left.

"Nothing would be better than my brother and best friend falling in love."

Nicole—always the romantic.

"Then you can tell me all about it." Nicole offered a feeble smile. "Just like best friends do."

Because the date was so important to her best friend and the only item left on Nicole's short bucket list, Irelynn had agreed.

IRELYNN PUT the twins to bed and sat on the couch for a long time, snuggled under a throw blanket. This year's April had been cooler than usual, and she couldn't wait for spring to officially arrive. She opened the worn envelope in her hand and retracted a folded letter.

Pressing out the creases, Irelynn stared at the precise handwriting of her best friend. The letter was to be opened after Nicole's death, and Irelynn estimated she had read it at least 15 times since then.

Dear Irelynn,

Thank you for helping take care of the twins while I was seeking treatment and during my frequent stays in the hospital. Knowing Mia and Max were well taken care of and provided for made the process easier to endure. I never could have gotten through those times without you.

Never did I imagine I'd get cancer. Didn't we always talk about the fact that we were such crazy health freaks? The doctors said there was a chance I'd win this battle, but if you are reading this letter, then I succumbed to the disease.

I know that we discussed after my cancer diagnosis who would care for Mia and Max in the event I didn't make it. At the time, it seemed like the "plan b of the plan b of the plan b" and inconceivable that custody arrangements would need to be considered, let alone made. You were always so reassuring that you would help to raise Mia and Max as your own should the unthinkable happen. You have already been such an important part of their lives and I thank you for that.

As we also discussed, my personal preference is that, if at all possible, the children would not be enrolled in day care.

I know you and Quinton will do fine sharing custody of the twins. I always, not so secretly, hoped that the two of you would end up liking each other and start dating, hence my reason for setting up your "blind date." That's the matchmaker in me, I suppose. A girl can always hope her brother and best friend get together, right? You two would truly make a cute couple.

Please give the custody arrangement a year to work out the kinks and to be sure Quinton isn't going to be deployed so soon after my death. After that year, please feel free to come to an agreement between the two of you that benefits, first and foremost, Mia and Max. I want you both to be in their lives and to raise them.

Please don't let the twins forget Tom and me. We both loved them so much. I remember the day I told Tom he was going to be a dad. Never had anything made him happier. If only he'd had the chance to meet them.

Take care, my dear friend, and know that had I not believed you could do it, I would not have insisted you become Mia and Max's second mom.

Much love,
Nicole

Irelynn folded the letter and placed it back in the envelope. She missed her best friend so much. Besides Mom, there had been no one Irelynn entrusted with her deepest secrets and hurts. She wiped the tears that filled her eyes, then kneeled by the edge of the sofa. Clasping her hands together, she prayed. For Mia and Max and their grief, for her own grief, and even for Quinton's grief. She prayed her finances would be enough to provide for her new family members. Then she prayed that God would give her the strength and ability to raise the twins.

When she finished her prayer, Irelynn sat on the floor and hugged her knees to her chest. Somehow, someway, she would succeed at the most important thing Nicole had ever asked of her.

To be a mom to her two children.

$\mathcal{I}$relynn and Mom found their usual place in the second row from the back on the far right-hand side of Chokecherry Heights Fellowship Church. She set the special bag of "goodies" she kept specifically for church on the seat next to her and anticipated the twins' arrival. She missed them when they stayed with Quinton.

Within minutes, Quinton, his grandmother, Mia, and Max filed into the same row. "Aunt Irelynn!" The twins ran toward her, arms outstretched, and she caught them in a hug. Tears misted her eyes. She couldn't bear the thought of not being a part of their lives.

"How was Uncle Quinton's?"

Mia's eyes grew round. "We ate tater chips."

Max nodded in agreement.

"Potato chips?"

"For dinner," Mia added.

Irelynn caught Quinton's eye. Figures that he'd feed them an unhealthy dinner. Quinton shrugged. "I didn't have any other snacks, so we had potato chips for movie night."

His grandmother took a seat next to him. Mia and Max

plopped between Irelynn and Quinton. Irelynn stretched out her arm and placed it around Max. He snuggled next to her.

The congregation joined in the first song, followed by Pastor Rehart's encouragement to greet each other.

"Irelynn," Quinton said, extending his hand.

God had a sense of humor, Irelynn thought wryly, that she had to shake hands with her somewhat-of-a-nemesis. "Quinton." His long fingers encompassed her smaller hand. Not that she was noticing he had long fingers.

"Hello, Irelynn, dear," said Quinton's grandmother.

"Hello, Mrs. Gregory."

"Oh, my, but do call me Gram. I haven't been called Mrs. Gregory since I worked at the library a lifetime ago."

Irelynn laughed. The petite woman with a Southern accent seemed to possess a pleasing personality, unlike her grandson. "Gram it is, then. And you remember my mother, Cynthia Brady?"

Mom turned from visiting with the overly-friendly Mr. Wilson in the back row and shook Gram's hand. They chatted briefly before Pastor Rehart began announcements.

After several more songs and the offering, the children were dismissed for children's church. "I'll take them this time," Mom offered.

"Are you sure?"

"Absolutely."

Each twin grabbed a hand and left with Mom. Irelynn looked up to see a man with a teenage boy tapping Quinton on the shoulder. "Excuse me," he said to Quinton and Gram, "but would you mind moving down so my son and I could sit with the rest of our family at the end of the row?"

Quinton scooted down the two seats that were formerly Mia's and Max's, until he sat right next to Irelynn.

Just great.

When she looked over at him, he gave her a sarcastic smirk.

She ignored him and instead opened her Bible to the passage Pastor had indicated.

Quinton was so close that Irelynn could smell the scent of his aftershave, a light, pleasing, woodsy scent. *The only thing pleasing about Quinton Gregory.*

Irelynn took notes on the provided sheet of paper. She finished writing the latest note from the overhead screen, then clicked her pen on and off while she listened to Pastor's sermon. A nervous habit, Irelynn supposed, but it had taken her some time to perfect the art of learning how to click the pen without making a sound. Suddenly and without warning, the pen flipped from her hand onto the floor in front of her. She leaned forward to retrieve it.

So did Quinton.

At the same time.

His arm brushed against hers as they both attempted to reclaim the pen. A tingly feeling settled into Irelynn's stomach. Her hand met his as they both grabbed the pen. She held her breath and let go of her hold on the writing utensil.

Finally, he turned to face her. "Here's your pen," he whispered, his face close to hers and his eye contact persistent.

Irelynn snatched the pen and sat back up in her chair. Heat burned her cheeks. What was it about Quinton? She didn't like him, so why did she get flustered at times around him? He was her somewhat-of-a-nemesis, after all.

She settled back and continued to listen to the sermon, hoping next week they could once again sit at opposite ends of the row.

And that she could leave her fumble fingers at home.

Quinton struggled to keep his mind on Pastor's words. Retrieving the pen for Irelynn had caused his thoughts to scatter.

What was wrong with being a gentleman and fetching it for her? Yet, the way she looked at him gave him cause to believe she didn't appreciate his chivalry.

But that pretty blush had crept up her face again. He was getting rather accustomed to how it made her green eyes brighten. Quinton really needed not to be thinking about her eyes —or her at all. *Remember...this is Irelynn Brady we're talking about here. The woman who wasn't responsible enough to show up at a pre-arranged date, especially for Nicole.*

"I'll go get Mia and Max," he heard Irelynn say. Before he could respond, she bolted from the sanctuary.

Her mother was speaking with that chummy Wilson guy in the back row, and Gram was involved in a conversation with the woman to her right. A few minutes later, Gram said to him, "How about I take us all to lunch?" She paused, as if knowing exactly what Quinton was going to say. "And, Quinton, I am treating."

He could argue with Gram all he wanted, but he would never win. "Sure."

"I'll ask Cynthia, and why don't you ask Irelynn?"

Something about the sparkle in Gram's eye when she made the suggestion didn't sit well with him. Something akin to indigestion. She was just as bad as Nicole when it came to her crazy matchmaking schemes. Hadn't she learned the last time when she attempted to set him up with the cook at the assisted living home's granddaughter? That had been a flop from the second it started.

Quinton shuffled his way through the aisle and out the door. He could catch Irelynn as she retrieved the twins from children's church. He doubted she would say "yes" to him. He should have suggested Gram ask her. No one turned down an offer from Gram.

Irelynn and the twins were nowhere to be found at the children's church room, so Quinton pivoted and walked the opposite direction.

After a time, he heard some rowdy noises coming from the partially empty hall. Mia and Max, running fast and acting far more rambunctious than usual, tore down the corridor, nearly colliding with several older folks.

"Mia and Max, please come here." Quinton heard Irelynn's voice before he saw her.

Of course, the two ignored her. They had really been struggling with naughtiness at his place the night before, so their continued disobedience didn't surprise him. They also hadn't slept well last night on their new toddler beds. Was this the result of that?

He strolled toward the children and caught them as they slammed into him. "Whoa, where are you going so fast?"

A few people gave Quinton a knowing glance, as if they knew exactly what it was like to raise rowdy children. Irelynn rushed toward them, her long pink skirt flowing around her ankles. "Mia and Max, I told you we never run in church."

Max pouted and Mia looked obstinate. Those two could be a handful at times. Quinton shook his head and looked at Irelynn. How were they ever supposed to raise them successfully? He didn't know the first thing about kids.

In response to his frustration, Irelynn narrowed her eyes at him, but said nothing. What was she thinking? Did she blame him for their behavior because he'd had them last night?

Quinton cleared his throat. There was no way to understand this odd woman, and he shouldn't even try. "Gram would like to take us all to lunch."

"Hmmm." She pressed her lips together in a thin line.

"Is that a 'yes' or a 'no'?"

"We want to go to lunch!" demanded Mia, with a stomp of her foot.

"Yeah, lunch," echoed Max.

"You two are in trouble."

Irelynn appeared to agree with his statement and nodded her head slightly, although she said nothing.

"Well?"

"What did Mom say?"

"I'm not sure. I left to come find you and the kids so I didn't hear her answer."

"If Mom agrees, I'll go. For Gram."

The last part of her statement was not lost on him. Of course, she didn't care to be in his presence any longer than necessary. The feeling was mutual.

Would she even show up?

Gram walked toward them with Cynthia. "There you two are. I can't wait to take you all to this new restaurant I discovered. It opened just last week."

"I hear it has phenomenal service," added Cynthia.

The decision was made then, and it didn't look like Irelynn Brady was happy about it one bit.

Snobby woman anyway.

IRELYNN RUBBED her temples in an effort to ease the headache that had begun to form ever since Mia's and Max's tirade at church. She then started her car and followed Mom, who followed Quinton. Was lunch at the restaurant really necessary? She wanted nothing more than a long nap.

Mom and Gram seemed to click. Irelynn had never known her grandma. Mom said she and Grandpa had disowned Mom when she eloped with Dad. Did Mom miss what could have been with her own mother? Did Gram in some way fill that void?

One thing was certain...Irelynn's accepting Gram's invitation had only to do with Mom's agreeing to go and with Irelynn thinking highly of Gram. Otherwise, she wouldn't be putting herself in Quinton's path again today. It was bad enough she'd have to see him tomorrow when he came to work on the remodel.

And who knew how many times during the week after that?

Besides, what was up with his judgmental attitude toward her when Mia and Max decided to dash through church like wild, untamed ruffians? She had seen him shake his head at the situation. Did Quinton think she was a terrible mom? Could he do any better?

She doubted it.

Especially a man who feeds children potato chips for dinner.

Gram's restaurant discovery was called Sutherland's Fine Dining. The older woman beamed when they were all seated at a booth in the corner. "This is such a delightful place. Wait until you taste the meatloaf." She and Mom, who sat next to each other to the right of Irelynn, engaged in conversation about anything and everything.

Irelynn adjusted the two booster seats between her and Quinton for the twins. After some squabbling, they each settled into a seat and began to color with the complimentary crayons.

The waiter introduced himself as Sam and began with Gram on the end, who ordered meatloaf. He then went to Quinton, since Mom was still browsing the menu. "And for your lovely wife?" asked Sam, smiling at Irelynn.

Irelynn cringed. From the corner of her eye, she saw Quinton grimace.

His lovely wife?

She'd rather own a spider pet shop than marry Quinton. And she detested spiders, not to mention, feared them.

Should Irelynn set Sam straight?

Best not to make a spectacle.

She cleared her throat. "I'll take the grilled chicken sandwich."

"And for your children?"

"Chicken nuggets! Chicken nuggets!" squealed Mia.

"Kickin' nuggets," echoed Max, in his unique childlike accent that Irelynn doubted Sam understood.

"How do we ask for things?" Irelynn asked.

Mia stared at the ceiling looking thoughtful, then piped up, "With a magic word."

Irelynn pointed toward Sam. "What is the magic word you should say to the waiter when asking for what you would like for lunch?"

"Please chicken nuggets?" asked Mia.

"Thank you?" questioned Max.

"Yes, that is right." She squeezed the children in a side hug, then looked up to see Quinton looking at her. Irelynn couldn't determine the expression in his eyes.

Best not to waste time even pondering what could be going through his mind.

"You're doing a wonderful job," said Mom. "It's not easy to instill manners in children."

"Oh, my, if that isn't the truth. When my son was a youngster, I felt like a broken record." Gram paused, a concerned expression in her squinty eyes. "Quinton, you and Irelynn do know what a broken record is, don't you?"

"Yes, Gram, we do. I saw one in a museum once."

Gram pointed her finger at Quinton. "Now, now, young man," she teased in response to his retort.

Mom placed her order for chicken salad, and Sam scribbled the order on his notepad. "I'll have your order right out," he said, all but forgotten by those from whom he had just taken lunch orders.

The food arrived and Quinton blessed the meal. At first, mealtime began as a peaceful event.

Until the most distressing thing that could happen did happen.

It all began with Max reaching a chubby finger toward Mia's plate and snatching one of her chicken nuggets.

Mia wailed, as if the fancy restaurant was on fire.

And then, things went from bad to worse. Much worse.

Max threw Mia's chicken nugget at the couple sitting at the next table. With surprisingly accurate aim, the nugget landed in the man's coffee.

Quinton appeared as though he wasn't sure he should clap at the possibility of Max's future athletic ability as a basketball star or reprimand him.

Mom tossed her sternest "mom look" toward the twins.

Gram covered her mouth with her hand. "Oh, y'all," she gasped.

And Irelynn pondered whether she should hide under the table and pretend she didn't know these people.

QUINTON SCOOPED UP MAX, and Irelynn reached for Mia. They carried the screaming, kicking toddlers out of the restaurant. Past Sam, who didn't look them in the eye; past the extravagant water fountain; past the crusty looks of several of the patrons; and to the freedom of the outdoors.

They stood to the side of the restaurant in a grassy area, made sloshy-wet from the recent rain. Quinton had no idea being a father would be this difficult. Dad had made it look so easy. He offered a silent prayer, then reprimanded Mia and Max for their behavior.

Mia's lip quivered and tears filled her large blue eyes. Max hid his face in Irelynn's skirt. The twins had been through so much trauma in losing their mother in the past month. Then going to live in two different places with two different people. How could they remain unscathed with all the changes they had faced?

She nestled against his shoulder. "What do we do?" he asked, not meaning for the words to be said aloud. The last thing he needed was for Irelynn to think he was incompetent.

Irelynn shrugged, then followed Quinton's lead and reached for Max. As she lifted him, Quinton saw a giant BBQ sauce stain he'd left behind on her pink skirt.

This parenting gig was more than either of them had bargained for.

Quinton led Irelynn to an outdoor bench and encouraged her to sit. He then sat beside her.

Moments passed with only the sound of sniffles from the twins and cars driving on the nearby road.

"They can't act like that in public. First the church and now the restaurant? They'll be terrors by the time they're five."

"And we'll be banned from all churches and all restaurants in a manner of months."

Quinton thought about laughing at her comment, but realized the possibility. He'd just started reviving the family business. He didn't need a bad reputation, nor did he need to uproot the twins and move to another town because they were no longer welcome in any public place in Chokecherry Heights.

Dad always said consistency was the key, and he and Mom had done consistency well. But would he and Irelynn ever be on the same page when it came to raising the twins?

He doubted it. They couldn't agree on anything, much less the upbringing of Mia and Max. They sat in uncomfortable silence; the children asleep in their arms. The aroma of food lingered in the air.

Reminding Quinton he'd had exactly one bite of his steak.

"It all started at the church. They shouldn't have been allowed to run around like that." He hadn't meant to muse aloud. As soon as he uttered the words, Quinton instantly regretted them.

"Are you insinuating that I wasn't watching the children?"

"Not at all. I'm just saying that they were starting to act up even at church." He tried to keep his voice low to avoid waking the twins, but success was not on his side. Max began to whimper.

Irelynn narrowed her eyes at him. "So, Mia and Max are never naughty when they stay with you?"

"I didn't say that."

"You didn't have to. You're implying that it's my fault they were bratty at church."

Quinton shook his head. "No, I didn't. You're misunderstanding me. I'm just saying that if they had behaved at church, maybe they would have been in a better frame of mind here at the restaurant."

"Or maybe, just maybe, if you hadn't fed them potato chips for dinner and allowed them to stay up so late, maybe they would have been better behaved at church and the restaurant."

"I didn't feed them potato chips for dinner. It was a snack during our movie night."

Irelynn tossed him a doubtful look. "And anyway, I saw you shaking your head when you saw them running through the hall, as if thinking I didn't know how to care for them."

"What?" Quinton couldn't remember shaking his head, nor thinking she didn't know how to care for the twins. The thought hadn't crossed his mind. "If I thought that, why would I let you have joint custody of them in the first place?"

"Let me?" Irelynn's eyes grew larger. She clearly was not happy with his choice of words. Leave it to him to make a bigger mess of the already-messy day. "Let's see," she continued, "because it was Nicole's wish?"

"Nicole wasn't thinking straight." That too, had come harsher than Quinton intended. "She only wanted what was best for the twins, but surely there had to be a better way than this mess."

Irelynn pursed her lips. "You're right, she wasn't thinking straight, and yes, this is a mess. It might be easier if you were easier to deal with."

"The feeling is mutual, Irelynn. You're about the most difficult person I've ever met."

"And *you* are the most arrogant, irritating, and disagreeable individual I have ever been forced to endure."

Quinton clenched his teeth. "Forced to endure? Since when do you have to endure me? I'm actually doing *you* a favor by helping you with the remodel."

"Oh really. At what cost?"

So much for gratitude. "Look, this is getting us nowhere. We need to just load up the kids and get them home. It's been a long day."

"Too long."

"Far too long." Had it been absolutely necessary they have lunch after church? Seeing Irelynn once in a day was enough. Tomorrow he'd see her again, and then probably the whole entire week while he worked on the rooms. Today could have been such a nice break from crossing paths with her for more than just church.

Thanks, Gram.

CHAPTER 6

Fortunately, Quinton said nothing to Irelynn except offering an obligatory head nod or muttered "hellos" when he came over on Monday, Tuesday, and Wednesday to measure and work on the rooms. It was for the best after their argument at Sutherland's Fine Dining on Sunday.

Irelynn made a mental note to never attend lunch with His Royal Arrogance again. Even if Gram requested it.

On Thursday, as was always the case any day he came over, Quinton lifted the twins into his arms. They planted a kiss on each cheek, and this time Irelynn snapped a picture with her phone. Why, she wasn't sure. Maybe to convince herself that while Quinton filled every guideline for being her somewhat-of-a-nemesis, he did have a soft side, one he showed with his niece and nephew. So maybe the guy was only 99 percent nemesis instead of 100 percent.

An optimist by nature, she did her best to remain positive.

But still, the less time she had to be in Quinton's presence, the better.

She stared at the picture on her phone, noting how much the twins resembled their uncle. They were fortunate to have a father figure in their lives who loved and cared for them. Having no dad in the picture had been hard for her in her younger years.

Still, if only Nicole had lived...

Quinton appeared to be inhaling the smell of baking cookies. Perhaps, just perhaps, if he kept his rude comments to himself, Irelynn would graciously present him with one of her award-winning cookies.

Irelynn giggled to herself. Award-winning because when she was in junior high, Mom had created a homemade certificate, had written "The Best Cookies Ever Award" in fancy writing, and had presented it to Irelynn.

The buzzer on the old stove sounded, and Irelynn rushed to the oven. The appliance that had come with the home when she purchased it had seen better days and had a habit of burning things left within its interior for even a brief moment longer than necessary. She pulled out a cookie sheet with a dozen perfectly-formed chocolate chip cookies.

"Are you two ready to deliver some cookies to Mrs. Caruthers?" she asked the twins.

"Who's Mrs. Ruthers?" Mia asked.

"She's our next-door neighbor. I thought it would be kind to take her some of the cookies."

Mia placed her hands on her hips. "Can we have one? And Uncle Quinton, can he have one too?"

"Let's take a plate over to Mrs. Caruthers, and then we'll have a tea party when we get back."

Hopefully Quinton would be long gone by then.

Max clapped his hands together and squealed. "Me like cookies," he said.

Irelynn reached for the spatula and placed three cookies on a blue plate. She glanced up and caught Quinton's eye. He gave a her a half-smile. Was he attempting to butter her up so she'd share some of the bounty?

Not a chance. It will take more than a half-hearted grin.

However, as quickly as his half-smile had appeared, it disappeared, and he resumed working to divide the room into two.

Such a peculiar sort you are, Mr. Gregory.

"Are you ready?" she asked the twins. They nodded and followed her out the door and over to Mrs. Caruthers's house.

The day would have been pleasant if it weren't for the wind that whipped through the trees. The clouds overhead signaled rain might be on the way.

One of these days, we'll be able to go for a run, Irelynn thought. She couldn't wait to use the new baby jogger Mom had surprised her with before Mia and Max were too big for it.

As they stepped onto Mrs. Caruthers's porch, Irelynn saw the elderly woman inside the house by a lamp. In her less-than-three months of living on Whitmore Street, Irelynn hadn't yet formally met the woman.

Mrs. Caruthers appeared to be jotting something down in her notebook, her gray spikey head nodding up and down as she did so and her glasses perched on her pointed nose. Was there ever a time when the woman wasn't scribbling something down in her notebook?

"Can I wing the doorbell?" Mia asked, her pudgy hand attempting to reach the glowing oval button.

"Yes, you may." Irelynn juggled the plate of cookies in one hand and lifted Mia with her other arm. Mia dinged the doorbell, not once, not twice, but three times, eliciting a giggle from Max.

"Ding again!" he squealed, encouraging his sister to ring the doorbell three more times.

Irelynn was just about to reprimand them when she noticed Mrs. Caruthers place her notebook on the table and peer out the window at them with a crusty expression. Hardly the impression Irelynn wanted to make when meeting her neighbor for the first time.

"What do you want?" Mrs. Caruthers asked when she opened the door.

Irelynn presented the plate of cookies, still warm from the oven. "We wanted to bring you some homemade cookies.

"How do you know I like cookies?"

"We just assumed everyone likes homemade cookies."

"Should you be assuming?" Mrs. Caruthers took the cookies from Irelynn.

"You can eat one," Mia informed her.

"I just might do that." Mrs. Caruthers stood in the doorway and took a nibble at one of the cookies. Her brown eyes widened to twice their size. "They are tasty."

"Thank you. By the way, I'm Irelynn Brady, and this is Mia and Max."

Mrs. Caruthers didn't invite them in, but instead took a few steps forward and inched herself through the front door to join them on the porch. "I'm Joyce Caruthers, president of the Neighborhood Lookout Society here on Whitmore Street."

Irelynn hadn't even realized there was a Neighborhood Lookout Society, but the thought was comforting. Sarcastically, she wondered if perhaps she should relay to Quinton that the children were safe in their new neighborhood, just in case he had concerns. "That's reassuring to know there's a watch program in place."

"Yes, well, not everyone you meet has laudable intentions." Mrs. Caruthers took another nibble of the cookie.

"It seems like a nice neighborhood from what I've seen so far."

"Most people are pleasant. Some, not so much. By the way, I've noticed that your handsome young fellow comes to visit quite often. What is the name of your young man?"

Her young man? Irelynn knew her face must be bright red from the warmth that traveled up her cheeks. "He's not..."

"Handsome young fellow," giggled Mia, repeating it two more times, and each time letting the words roll off her tongue.

"It appears he is somewhat handy from what I have gleaned. Of course, working for that Gregory Construction outfit, he best be. I saw the name of the company on the side of his truck." Mrs. Caruthers paused and held her head high. "It's all part of the job to be observant, that's why it's not a job for just anybody."

"Yes, he's the owner of the company."

"Ooh," Mrs. Caruthers exclaimed, her eyes enlarging once again beneath her thick glasses. "A handsome young fellow *and* the owner of his own company. You've done well for yourself, Mrs. Brady."

"It's not..." *what you think!*

"Never you mind. At first, I thought he was your husband, except that he comes and goes far too often for that. Sometimes with the children, sometimes not. Is he your ex-husband? Perhaps the two of you are attempting to reunite after some time apart?"

Irelynn was speechless. Mrs. Caruthers thought Quinton was her ex-husband? *That was definitely an offensive comment. Never in my worst nightmares would I be married to Quinton Gregory.* Besides, was there nothing this woman *didn't* know about the ongoings of the neighborhood?

As if she read Irelynn's thoughts, Mrs. Caruthers continued. "You may wonder why I know so much about you and your handsome young fellow. It's part of my job as the president of the Neighborhood Lookout Society. I report all suspicious activity to the police department."

"I feel safer just knowing you're here."

"As well you should. Two other people competed for this role, and I won. It wasn't easy, but I knew we needed someone who would devote their time and efforts into such a worthwhile cause and not forsake the necessity of keeping watch over this splendid neighborhood. A neighborhood I myself have lived in for the past 40 years. Why, when Mr. Hill and Mrs. Potter both decided to run for the position, I knew they wouldn't come close to fulfilling the necessary obligations that I vow to uphold." Her eyes darted toward her house and at the notebook sitting on the table.

Were all of her observations recorded in the purple notebook?

"We should be returning home. It was nice to meet you, Mrs. Caruthers."

"And you as well. I would be remiss if I didn't add that whatever your differences are, you and your husband should reunite posthaste. The dear children need their parents to be unified."

Husband? Why did it seem like the air had gotten thinner and that her breathing had become labored? "Mrs. Caruthers, Quinton..."

"Quinton? There now, I'll have to remember that name. Quinton Brady—the handsome young fellow." Mrs. Caruthers tossed a glance toward the purple notebook.

"Handsome young fellow," chirped Mia.

Max giggled.

"Mrs. Brady, one thing you'll notice about me is I am not the chatty type. I prefer to leave well enough alone, and I savor my privacy, so once a month is more than enough to visit."

"I'll remember that."

"Yes, and say hello to your handsome young fellow."

"Handsome young fellow," Mia repeated once more, as if she was a parrot.

Mrs. Caruthers waved goodbye and stepped back inside her house.

"Let's get back home so we can have our tea party," Irelynn told Mia and Max. She took one last glance back at Mrs. Caruthers and noticed the woman sitting at her table furiously scribbling something in the notebook.

She cringed at what the woman may have written.

WHEN THEY RETURNED HOME, Irelynn put Mia and Max to work passing out toy dishes in the form of plates, cups, and a teapot on the table. "Can Uncle Quinton come to the tea party?" Mia asked.

Irelynn doubted very much that Quinton would want to

attend a tea party, but she nodded, and Mia ran toward the room. "Uncle Quinton, come have a tea party."

Quinton stood and dusted his pants off in the "construction zone" before walking across the floor to the rest of the house. "I haven't ever been to a tea party before," he said, his eyes glistening. Was that emotion she saw in them?

"Then you have to come." Mia took one hand, and Max took the other, and they dragged him to the table. He appeared to enjoy every minute of it. Mia pointed to one of the chairs. "You sit here," she demanded.

"You sit," echoed Max.

"Aunt Irelynn, you sit here." Mia patted the chair directly next to Quinton, and Irelynn wanted to object, but she refrained. "Max, you sit here, and I'll sit here," continued Mia. The two climbed into their booster seats while Irelynn passed out the cookies and set the miniature teapot with punch on the table.

"Say pwayers," said Max, bowing his head. "Tank You, God, for cookies. Amen."

After prayers, Mia suggested that Quinton pour the punch. Irelynn watched as he attempted to maneuver the teapot. His shoulder brushed hers as he poured the punch into her tiny teacup. Something jolted inside her stomach, and Irelynn ignored it. When he finished, Irelynn brought the cup to her lips and took the one sip that was contained within it.

Just at that moment, Mia announced, "He's your handsome young fellow. That's what Mrs. Ruthers said."

Irelynn choked and nearly spit out the sip of punch. While Mia had parroted that phrase after Mrs. Caruthers had mentioned it, Irelynn never imagined her to do it in Quinton's presence.

"What was that, Mia?" Quinton asked, his blond eyebrows knitted together.

Mia giggled and pointed from Quinton to Irelynn. "He's your handsome young fellow."

Not my handsome young fellow, Irelynn wanted to announce, but the words wouldn't come. As a matter of fact, no words would come. Rather, a strange noise emitted from her vocal cords. Her throat felt like it might close and she might choke. Or gag. Could she just die right now and get it over with?

She avoided Quinton's stare in her direction. Did he think...

When her eyes finally met his, she saw amusement mixed with horror in their depths. And he sat too close. Far too close. *Thanks a lot, Mia, for sitting us side by side.* Not that there was much room at the humble kitchen table. Irelynn struggled to find her voice. A raspy tone emerged. "Uh, Mrs. Caruthers thought you were my handsome young fellow. Of course, I tried to set her straight. I mean, really, the thought itself is appalling to say the least. You as my handsome young fellow." Irelynn resisted the urge to shiver for dramatic effect. "Who even talks like that anyway?"

"Appalling is right," Quinton agreed. "You couldn't pay me enough to be your 'handsome young fellow.' Mrs. Caruthers must not be as observant as she thinks."

"She *is* the president of the Neighborhood Lookout Society."

"Mrs. Caruthers should brush up on her surveillance skills or she'll never graduate to the FBI." Quinton took another cookie from the plate in the center of the table. "These aren't half bad."

Half bad? Did the man have no sense of taste? These were award-winning cookies. Just ask Mom.

CHAPTER 7

Quinton hadn't tasted homemade cookies this delicious since Mom used to make them when he was a teenager. He'd invite all of his friends over, and they'd devour two entire batches just in time for supper. But he wouldn't let Irelynn know what he really thought.

Speaking of thoughts on a matter...Mrs. Caruthers, that strange neighbor, thought he and Irelynn were a couple? If only she knew there was no way he'd ever see Irelynn in that light.

He could barely tolerate her.

She was a partner in the parenting of Mia and Max, but that was it.

Quinton envisioned their lives a few years from now. They would be agreeing to meet for all sorts of events in which the children participated. Would she bother showing up?

Reining in his sarcastic thoughts, he instead thought of the past few days.

Irelynn had barely said two words to him this entire week when he came over to work on the renovation. If it weren't for the twins, he'd much rather be working on one of his other projects. Things were about to improve in his life, though, when in a few weeks, the hired electrician would come and wire the new rooms. That would give Quinton a much-needed break from his daily visits. He would miss the twins, but that was it.

He poured himself another miniature cup of punch. "I won't be here tomorrow to work on the renovation, but my next plan is to frame in the studs for the wall between the rooms. I'll pick the kids up tomorrow night." His voice sounded to his ears like a robot on a science fiction show.

"That's fine."

Fine by him, too.

"I'll pick up my tools and be on my way." Tonight was the night he visited Gram at the assisted living home. He glanced at his fitness tracker for the time. If he hurried, he'd be on time to join her and her friends for a game of Uno, which was important to Gram.

And though he wouldn't admit it to anyone else, it was important to Quinton as well.

Elderly Mrs. Pierce motioned to Quinton to sit at the table. "Well, hello, young man. Care to join us for a game of cards? We were just starting a new round, and we need a fourth player since Milt just left."

"Sure. Hello, Gram, ladies." Quinton placed a kiss on Gram's cheek and took a seat next to her.

"How have you been this week?"

"Busy."

Gram smiled at him and dealt the cards. "I just love Uno," squealed Miss Bea, a round jolly sort with oversized pop-bottle glasses that illuminated her already enormous brown eyes.

Quinton figured they all loved Uno, since that's what they played each Wednesday when he came to visit.

"Have you found yourself a wife yet?" Mrs. Pierce asked.

"It's time you found yourself a wife," added Miss Bea.

Who knew two 80-something-year-old women could be so nosy?

Gram patted Quinton on the shoulder. "Now, now, ladies, Quinton just hasn't found the right girl yet."

"There's a real nice gal who's the new night nurse. We ought to set them up," chortled Miss Bea.

Mrs. Pierce leaned forward in her chair. "No, not her. How about the secretary? Now there's a likeable gal."

Quinton shook his head. Why was everyone trying to always marry him off? First Mrs. Caruthers thinking he and Irelynn were a couple, and now Miss Bea and Mrs. Pierce playing matchmaker. For all they knew, he'd remain a bachelor until he was 95. Easier that way. "I'm content with things the way they are."

Gram had a suspicious glint in her squinty eyes. He was scared to even entertain what she might be thinking on the topic.

"There are so many lovely young women who would adore a young man such as yourself," declared Mrs. Pierce. She adjusted her glasses higher on her stubby nose. "Why, you are an accomplished Uno player, a construction worker, and so knowledgeable about the Bible. Remember that time Miss Bea and I quizzed you all the way from Genesis to Revelation?"

Oh, he remembered the "Bible Quiz" all right. How could he forget? It lasted three hours, and the only reward he received was an anemic piece of apple pie. And a construction worker? Poor Mrs. Pierce appeared confused. "Look, ladies, with all respect, I am content being a bachelor."

Miss Bea shook her finger at Quinton. "Now, now. That's what they all say, but some young woman will waltz into your life and you'll forget you ever uttered those words. Trust me. I know what I'm talking about."

Hadn't Gram told him that Miss Bea had never been married? Speaking of Gram, Quinton tossed her a pleading look. "Gram, can you help me out here? I'm outnumbered by the Matchmaker Society."

Gram giggled. "I agree with them, Quinton, so you're outnumbered for sure."

What a traitor.

~

AFTER EIGHT ROUNDS OF UNO, Quinton and Gram went to her apartment, where they sat and visited until dinner. "How is it going with the children?" Her Southern accent was still strong after all these years away from her hometown.

"It's tough, Gram. All of this shuffling back and forth between Irelynn and me. Mia and Max are struggling as it is."

Gram nodded. "I could see the challenge at the restaurant that Sunday after church. You both have your hands full, to be sure. If I remember correctly, Nicole said to give this arrangement a year, and then make plans to change it, if necessary, just as long as the children stay with you and Irelynn. She wished for you both to raise them."

"Yes." Quinton sighed. "We'll do that for Nicole. But, Gram, I have to say it's weird how Irelynn never did show up for that date Nicole arranged for us."

"Are you still nursing that old wound?" Gram asked.

Old wound? It was a bit over a month ago. Maybe his pride was *slightly* wounded. But whose wouldn't be when he sat at Fernandez's for an hour waiting for Irelynn. It would be some time before he would want to see nachos and salsa again after devouring two baskets of the complimentary appetizers while waiting for his supposed date. Everyone had stared at him with pity in their eyes, many whom he knew from living here so long. The waitress had asked him three times if he'd meant to ask for a table for one instead of a table for two.

Quinton didn't even want to think about the whole sitting there by himself thing. Tough on anyone, but especially an extrovert.

"She should have called," he muttered. "Or texted."

"True. But why don't you ask Irelynn why she didn't arrive at the restaurant. She probably has a valid reason."

Quinton shifted. "I'll tell you, though, Gram, Irelynn isn't the easiest person to talk to."

"How so?"

"She's...let's put it this way...have you ever met someone who just rubs you the wrong way, so to speak?"

Gram laughed and placed a wrinkled hand on Quinton's arm. "Oh, my, yes. Haven't I ever told you about how your grandfather and I met?"

"I don't think so."

"He was the young pastor for the new Bible club for unchurched youth. Nowadays, such pastors are common, but back then, it was a new idea. Anyhow, from the moment I met him, I was determined not to like him. Not one bit."

"Really?"

"Really. You see, I wasn't always smitten with the man I grew to love more than anyone else on this earth." Gram paused and glanced at the picture of her and Gramps on the table beside the couch. "They put me in charge of helping out at the Bible club. When he first saw me, he thought I was one of the youngsters and didn't hesitate to treat me as such. Well, that festered me up some, seeing as how I was, at the ripe old age of 20, no youthful girl."

"Was it because of your size?" Gram had always been petite.

"That and because I've always looked young for my age. Still do," she snickered.

No humility there, Gram.

"But it all worked out in the end."

"It did. I grew to love him. Now, I'm not saying you will grow to love Irelynn because that's not always how God's plan works, but you could grow to like her. After all, you do have a common interest in raising the children."

"She's snobby, Gram."

"From the times I met her, I didn't figure her to be the type to put on airs. She always has seemed so sweet and amiable."

"Maybe to you. I can tell she doesn't like me any more than I like her."

"Just because you don't cotton to someone right away doesn't mean you won't like them at some point. Your grandfather and I were a perfect example of that."

"It's not going to be that way with Irelynn and me. We will probably become friendly acquaintances for Mia and Max, but we definitely won't come close to what you and Gramps were."

"Such a scowl on that handsome face of yours, Quinton. She's not that unpleasant, is she?" Gram paused. "She's a fine mother to the children, loves them and cares for them. What's there not to admire about her? Oh, and she's pretty."

"She might be some of those things, but...all right, all of them, but look, Gram, can we talk about something else?"

"Sure, Quinton. What else is going on? How is the remodel project?"

"Going slow, and I'll be glad when it's done. We just finished pouring the foundation for the second house over in the Waterbury Acres Subdivision. Next come the walls, and that goes fairly fast."

"I always was so proud of you, taking on your daddy's business like this. You would make him proud."

Quinton cleared his throat. If only Dad and Mom were here... He turned toward his grandmother. "Gram, I'm going to be purchasing a house in the near future. I would love to build one, but I need something I can move the kids into sooner rather than later. It's not working at the apartment. Don't get me wrong, I don't mind sleeping on the couch while having their beds set up in my room, but it's too cramped. And they need space to run and play."

"I agree."

"There are two homes for sale in my price range. One is over on Fourth Street. The other is down the street from Irelynn's. The one on Fourth Street looks well-maintained from what I saw when I drove by, while the one on Whitmore Street near Irelynn's needs a lot of work done, judging from the outside. Either way, I need something different than the apartment. I'm going to take a look at them both on Monday."

"Sounds like prayers are in order for the right decision."

"I'd appreciate that, Gram. I don't want to jump into anything too hastily. A house purchase is a big decision."

"The one on Fourth Street in better condition sounds appealing. However, the house down the street from Irelynn's. Hmmmm..." Gram let her Southern drawl extend more than usual with her musings.

"It would be convenient."

"Convenient indeed."

"Gram, are you teasing me?"

"I could be. Perhaps living closer to each other will cause you to be more amicable toward one another."

Quinton shrugged. "It will certainly be easier for the transfer of the twins. It needs a lot of work, though. But maybe for the right price, I could do what's necessary for us to move into it, then work on it while we live there." He paused. He hadn't even seen the interiors of the homes yet. Maybe he should wait until more options came on the market. "Irelynn's neighborhood seems like a nice one, except one woman who is always on her porch taking notes in a notebook. She thinks Irelynn and I are a couple. What's up with that, anyway?"

"You two would make a handsome couple."

Why did this disturbing topic always come up?

"Let's talk about something else, Gram. Back to the neighborhood. It's quiet and close to the running paths and the park."

"It sounds like the perfect place, both for a runner such as yourself, and for the children with the park and the sake of convenience. Is it reasonably priced?"

"Being on the market so long leaves room for negotiation and more likely in my price range. It'll be interesting to see what it looks like on the inside, and maybe I can make an offer. The Fourth Street house is further away and not in as desirable of a neighborhood, but it appears there's a lot less work to be done on it." Quinton paused. "Gram, why don't after I purchase a house, you move into it with me? Both are decent-sized houses."

Gram held his hand in a soft grasp. "Precious grandson of mine, I am perfectly content here at the assisted living home. Y'all know I'm a social butterfly and have to have my Uno games, Bible studies, and movie nights. Besides, you have two children to raise."

"But, Gram..."

"Now, now, I'm comfortable here. They treat me well and the cook makes the best collard greens and country ham dish I've ever tasted."

Quinton shook his head. Was there no winning with Gram? "If you're sure."

"I'm not only sure, but content. Besides, someday you'll want to take a wife."

"Not any time soon."

Gram's eyes sparkled. "We never know what the Lord has in mind now, do we?"

No, Quinton didn't know what the Lord had in mind. But he knew one thing...marriage was not something on Quinton's mind.

Quinton tossed one way, then the other on the couch, begging sleep to come. It had been a long day, as he finished up the remodel for Mrs. Jones right on schedule. He loved it when a plan came together like that.

But thoughts clouded his mind. Over and over. Guilt. Grief. Worry. Trepidation. Apprehension. He flipped the alarm clock toward him. Already 3:37 a.m. At least it was Saturday.

He sat up and peeked in on Mia and Max. Thankfully, they had fallen asleep soon after he'd put them to bed.

Quinton tiptoed into his bedroom and opened the bi-fold doors to his closet. He reached toward the top shelf for the olive green metal box with a lid. Holding the handle tightly in his grasp, Quinton carried it from the room and placed it on the kitchen table. He perched on the chair and flipped the "on" switch of the lantern he used for camping, so he wouldn't have to turn on the kitchen light. The last thing he wanted was to wake the twins.

Even before Quinton opened the box, memories flooded his mind. A mixed variety of recollections from as far back as he could remember. He fumbled with the clasp, flipped it up, and opened the top-mounted lid of Dad's ammo box that he'd had from his time in the military.

Two generations of veterans. Would Mia or Max follow in their footsteps?

The lantern flooded light into the box. Pictures mainly. But also his Medal of Honor, Mom's silver cross necklace that he kept someday for Mia, and the antique pocket watch Dad had given him that had belonged to Great-grandfather Gregory.

Quinton retrieved the Medal of Honor first. He rubbed his thumb over the gold-star award on the blue ribbon. His mind retreated back to that day when he'd pulled not one, but two men out of enemy fire.

One man lived.

One man died.

Emil had survived, although both legs had to be amputated. He had returned to his wife and children in Pennsylvania.

Tom hadn't survived. The horrific images of Tom's broken and bleeding body as Quinton carried him while dodging enemy fire would forever be ingrained in Quinton's mind.

Especially at times when he should be sleeping.

Quinton had risked his life that day to retrieve Tom and Emil. Not a thought of his own danger had entered his mind. Just a prayer asking God to go before him and hurried footsteps—as hurried as they could be with his own injuries.

"Tom, you can't die, man. You can't." Quinton leaned over Tom and begged his best friend to look at him. Tom stared, but didn't appear to see. "You can't die, man. God, please don't let him die! Look, Tom, I promised Nicole—promised her I'd keep you safe and bring you home to her. You have two babies now, so you can't go dying on me. Got that?"

Tom didn't respond. Quinton begged God several more times in rapid succession. Loud noises sounded all around him.

Safe from danger now, Emil stirred. Quinton glanced at him, but he'd not leave Tom's side. Not until he knew Tom would survive.

Felt for a pulse.

None.

Tom was gone.

Quinton unfolded a newspaper clipping with several creases marring the newsprint. His eyes scanned the headline and the subsequent article, even though he knew it by heart. *One U.S. Service Member Killed and Two Injured in Deadly Roadside Explosion.*

He had disappointed Nicole and failed to keep his promise.

The combat experience had left him with PTSD and extensive counseling. He still attended meetings once a month with other veterans at the VA in a city 100 miles away. Why he had received the Medal of Honor, he couldn't understand. He'd been prepared to do what any other man would do—what Jesus had done—to lay down his life for his friends. Quinton had given no thought to death that day when he'd pulled Tom and Emil from the wreckage.

It was an experience Quinton wouldn't wish on his worst enemy, but it *had* drawn him closer to God.

Quinton reached for the pocket watch and read again the inscription on the back. *To my beloved Quinn, much love, Bessie.* Great-grandmother Bessie had given the watch to Quinton's namesake, Great-grandfather Quinn Gregory. It had been passed on from generation to generation, and would someday be passed to Max.

Lastly, but most importantly, Quinton perused the photos. Several were from when he and Nicole were children. He swallowed hard. In those days, Quinton would never have fathomed she would die so young.

Or his parents. Family pictures also filled the box. Mom with her habitually smiling face and Dad smirking, as if he'd just played a trick on someone. The car crash that took them before they even had a chance to be grandparents.

Life wasn't fair.

If Quinton allowed himself to, he could get depressed. It all weighed so heavily on him.

Placing the items back inside the box, Quinton closed the lid, clasped the fastener, then returned it to its place in the closet.

The children rested peacefully in their beds.

This time, Quinton wouldn't let Nicole down. He'd do his best to raise the children just how she would want them raised.

Even if he had to deal with painful memories, the stress of reviving the business, and a woman named Irelynn Brady.

PROMPTLY AT 10:00 a.m. on Monday morning, Quinton drove to the house at 1446 Whitmore Street, a block from Irelynn's humble abode. He checked the foundation, the front yard landscaping, or lack thereof, and inspected the jagged crack in the driveway. Could he make this house livable for his new family?

He heard a door shut and noticed that Mrs. Caruthers had been walking her poodle down the street. She carried a notebook in one hand and held a leash in the other. He stared at her for a minute while she wrote some things down, looked up at him, then scribbled more notes. Quinton raised a hand to wave. With hesitation, Mrs. Caruthers lifted a hand to wave back. Such an odd woman.

While waiting for the real estate agent, Quinton moseyed around the yard. He lifted the latch on the wooden gate that had seen better days and stepped into the back yard. Overgrown weeds and a few pieces of trash littered the area. The fence, tilted down in some areas as if windblown, needed to be replaced. He took a step and nearly landed in dog feces.

How had the place not been condemned?

If Quinton wasn't able to make the place near new, there was no way he was allowing Mia and Max to live here. If he could get it for the right price and the remodel overhaul could be done reasonably, it might just work. Either way, after he saw inside, he'd pray and crunch numbers. There were other options if this wasn't doable.

Like the house on Fourth Street he'd go see later this afternoon.

He wandered back to the front yard just in time to hear a vehicle coming down the quiet street. An upscale black SUV pulled up in front of the house. Quinton didn't have to stand close to the vehicle to see the words plastered all over the back window: *Isabelle Vacura, Real Estate Agent. Don't hire me unless you want the best.*

Isabelle. He had known her since freshman year in high school and then later graduated with her. He hadn't seen her in all these years, which he was grateful for since she'd always carried a torch for him.

And he'd never felt the same.

She emerged from her black SUV, looking more as if she was on her way to attend a fancy gala than make a potential real estate transaction. Isabelle flipped her blonde hair over her shoulder and tossed a gleaming smile his way. Why couldn't someone else be the agent to meet him here? Didn't the sign say the listing agent was someone named Murray?

"Quinton!" She waved and strolled toward him.

He watched as she teetered on high heels. How could women wear those things, let alone walk in them? "Hi, Isabelle."

"I'm so happy to see you again. What's it been? Years?"

"Something like that." And he had no intentions of reliving those years with a woman whose flirting was giving him a headache.

"So, you're interested in buying this house? I'm sure with your construction skills, you'll be able to fix it so it looks brand new, and flip it with no problem at all. I happen to know a fabulous real estate agent for when that time comes." She winked at him.

Isabelle Vacura hadn't changed one bit since high school. "Thanks, Isabelle. For now, I'm just checking out my options."

"You were always a man of such wisdom," she gushed and flashed him another smile of perfectly straight white teeth, giving testimony that she was the daughter of a prominent orthodontist in town. "Wait until you see the inside. The former owner really did a number on it." Isabelle rolled her eyes. "Unfortunate how that happens sometimes, but it's been on the market over a year and is listed at an outstanding price—just enough for the relative who inherited it to get out from under it. You could really make it nice and sell it. Kind of like that house you and your dad did over on Eleventh Avenue back in the day."

"Maybe." Quinton remembered that house. A fixer-upper with almost no hope until Dad got a hold of it and taught Quinton everything there was to know that summer about remodeling a house from the ground up.

Isabelle twirled a piece of her hair between her finger and thumb and giggled. "You're amazing, Quinton, with what you can build. You'll do fantastical with this house. The new owner won't even know it was ever a dump."

He didn't bother telling her that if he did buy this house, Quinton would be keeping it as the home where he would raise Mia and Max. She came closer and placed her arm through his elbow. Quinton nearly choked at her brazenness and strong perfume. She sidled in closer. "So, Quinty..."

Quinty?

"Shall we go inside and check out the place?"

"Sure." Hopefully his voice held more enthusiasm than he felt.

Isabelle led him to the front door. Already, Quinton could tell the place needed work. A ton of it. Scratches, a dent, and a crack in the glass on the front door told him this house had been allowed to fall into disrepair.

The pungent smell of urine greeted them when they entered the house. "Apparently the former owner allowed the dogs to run around and live in here—all eight of them."

"Smells like it."

Isabelle giggled again. "Quinty, I love that you don't pull any punches on what you're thinking. We really need to get together sometime. You know, catch up."

That was the last thing Quinton wanted, but he didn't say so. He needed an exceptional deal on this house, not to offend Isabelle. Maybe he wasn't as upfront as she thought.

He peered out the numerous front windows. If they were replaced with new energy-efficient windows, it would be a considerable improvement. He noticed Irelynn briskly walking down the sidewalk with Mia and Max in a double jogger stroller. He stared for a moment, wishing he could go on a walk with them inside of being stuck inside the odor-ridden house with Isabelle the flirt.

Get a grip, Quinton. You two can't get along long enough to go for a walk.

Irelynn took off down the sidewalk in a jog. She was a runner?

Chalk one point up for Irelynn. A fellow runner couldn't be all that bad.

"Earth to Quinton." Isabelle waved a manicured hand in front of his face.

"Sorry."

"The living room could use some TLC and some serious odor elimination, don't you think?"

Quinton scanned the living room, complete with its popcorn ceiling, and wanted to cringe. It needed more than TLC. Dad would call this "the ultimate challenge." And as for the odor, the strongest air fresheners would fail.

His eyes traveled toward the galley kitchen. He could knock out that wall and...

Isabelle again looped an arm through his. "Come this way and let's look at the kitchen."

The kitchen boasted a kicked-in stainless steel refrigerator, a badly stained stove, and exposed wires where it appeared an old-fashioned portable dishwasher once resided. "Does this place have electrical issues?"

"Not sure. I can find out for you, though. The appliances are included."

"They'll just have to be hauled away in a dump run."

"A lot of work, but I'm sure you can do it, Quinty." She looked at him with adoring eyes.

He really hated it when she called him Quinty. "Look, Isabelle..."

"So, when you were gazing out that window, I saw you staring at that woman on the sidewalk with the stroller. Do you know her?"

"I do."

"I wondered. Kind of plain, don't you think?"

"What?"

Isabelle pooched her red-lipsticked lips at him. "She's kind of plain, don't you think? I mean what kind of woman dresses in workout gear during the day when she's not at the gym?"

"Maybe a woman who wants to take her kids on a run in the baby jogger? Why does it matter, Isabelle?"

And plain was not a word he would use to describe Irelynn.

"It doesn't. I just am all about fashion and looking classy. Come on, I'll show you the rooms."

Quinton followed her down the hall to the three bedrooms. If the living room and kitchen were bad, the rooms were horrific. Torn up carpet in places, holes in the walls, and two bathrooms with tubs so filthy they appeared never to have been cleaned.

If he purchased this house, and it was a big "if," Quinton would have his work cut out for him. The "ultimate challenge" for sure.

Isabelle led him to the basement. A musty odor permeated the threadbare carpeted stairs. He'd have to get the place checked out for mold. Having that would be a deal-breaker with Nicole's asthma and the possibility that one or both of the children had inherited it.

"Do you remember our high school days?" Isabelle cooed, interrupting Quinton's thoughts about mold remediation. "Hard to believe we've been out of high school for nine years."

"Yep. Time goes fast."

"You were on the track team and I cheered you on to victory. We made quite the team, don't you think?"

How was Quinton supposed to answer that? He didn't think they were a team at all. He liked Isabelle as a friend, but that was as far as it went for him, despite her hints and eagerness for them to take their friendship to the next level.

"We really should catch a play at the theater in the city."

"I'm really not into plays, Isabelle."

"Oh." She stuck her lower lip out into a pout. "You'd go see one for me, though, right?"

"I'm not into plays."

Isabelle relented in her pestering him about plays, and Quinton let out a sigh of relief. Right now, he had to focus on raising the twins and finding a more suitable place for them to live. Even if he did like Isabelle in that way, which he didn't, finding time for a relationship was next to impossible at this stage of his life.

Unless the perfect girl came along...

What? Why did Gram's voice and a suggestion just like what she would utter ram through his mind just then? No, not even the perfect girl. He had too much going on: the kids, the business, grief over Nicole, and guilt over Tom's death. There was no time for even the perfect girl.

"Quinty? Are you all right?" Isabelle's looming face stared at his.

"Just thinking is all."

"I always liked that about you—the strong and silent type, as they would say in the romance novels."

The last thing Quinton wanted to do was be like someone in a romance novel. He strolled through the basement, noting it was partially finished. That made things a lot easier. Ideas percolated through his mind. The spacious room would make an awesome family room. He envisioned the big screen TV against one wall, room for the twins' toys, and a big bean bag chair like what he had in his room as a teenager. He could renovate part of it into a home office.

"I don't see a bathroom down here, but you could put one in," said Isabelle, the heel of her shoe nearly snagging on the old green shag carpet. "For resale value, a house needs a bathroom on each level."

"I could easily plumb one in," he answered.

"So, what do you think? You could buy it and make a killing after fixing it up."

Or Quinton could buy it, pour money into it and give it a fresh makeover, and raise the twins in a home that would be theirs.

This could be doable...if he could get it for a bargain price.

CHAPTER 9

After putting the twins to bed, Irelynn retreated to the front porch. It had been a long day. She'd phone-interviewed for two at-home part-time positions, taken Mia and Max to the park, gone grocery shopping, and completed the one lone assignment Jamie had emailed her.

Irelynn thought about the unkempt house down the street that was for sale. She noticed Quinton had spent time there this morning. She'd observed him peering out the window when she took the twins to the park. Obviously, he was interested in purchasing it. A new remodel job perhaps? Just from its outer appearances, one would need to get an excellent deal on it just to break even with all the work that likely needed to be done on the inside. She'd never met the former owner, as Irelynn had moved in after the house went up for sale.

When Irelynn had returned from the park, Quinton and the real estate agent were in the front yard. He must be serious about the place if he'd spent over an hour there.

It also appeared Quinton knew the real estate agent quite well. The stylish woman seemed all too friendly with him, as close as she stood with her arm looped through his and her head tilted toward him.

Not that she was noticing.

But...was the real estate agent his girlfriend? Irelynn had never thought about the fact that he could have a girlfriend and what that would mean for the unorthodox custody arrangement.

A peculiar feeling churned in Irelynn's stomach. Why would she care whether Quinton had a girlfriend or not?

A light flickered in Mrs. Caruthers's house, and Irelynn noticed the woman through the curtains sitting at a desk, note-book in hand. *What I wouldn't give to take a peek inside that notebook.* What would it contain? Notes on her? The twins? Quinton? The rest of the neighbors? And what kind of notes would it include? Maybe she could set Mrs. Caruthers up with a website announcing her services as a private investigator. *Need to find out about that potential employee? Future boyfriend? Everything you ever needed to know about just about anyone tucked away inside a plain purple notebook. Call today for an appointment.*

Irelynn laughed then, thinking of how Mrs. Caruthers would make a perfect character in some book or on a television show. She welcomed the reprieve from the stress that permeated through her. Of course, just to be imagining a tagline for Mrs. Caruthers's website and the fact the woman could be in a book or movie lent truth to the fact that Irelynn was becoming delirious in her stressed state of mind.

She tugged the hoodie sleeves over her hands. The days had gotten warmer, but the nights still lent the chill of spring. At least she'd been able to run again. That always alleviated some stress. Irelynn gazed up at the stars. Would Nicole think she was doing a satisfactory job raising the twins so far? Irelynn tried her hardest to raise them in a way that would make Nicole proud.

If only you'd beat the cancer, Nicole. Life isn't fair.

Irelynn rose and went back inside. She needed to pay some

bills tonight while all was quiet. The computer screen indicated the truth about her current financial situation. Of course, she knew after last month what the outcome would be. Even with the amount of death benefits the children received from Tom's death and withdrawing money from her dwindling savings, she couldn't pay all of her bills. This month would be worse with the cut in her hours.

After she finished, Irelynn sat staring at the screen. What more could she cut? There was no way around the mortgage, electrical and water bills, and house and car insurance. She'd even raised her deductibles on the latter two and stretched her mortgage to 30 years. Unfortunately, when she'd become joint caregiver for the twins, she'd had to charge some items on her charge card for them. Then her computer had crashed, and there had been that extra expense. The car would need new tires soon, especially before next winter.

And then there was the remodel job. Quinton had already charged a substantial sum onto her account. She had to believe he was being frugal, but with money as tight as it was, Irelynn figured any amount would be too much. At least the Nathanson's account only required low monthly payments.

A whimper from one of the children sounded then, and she rose to check on them. It was Mia this time, and Irelynn leaned over and placed a kiss on her forehead. Mia stirred, but soon fell back asleep. She checked on Max and kissed his furrowed brow. Was he dreaming of a time when his mom was alive? And was it normal that he didn't speak nearly as much as Mia? Should she take him to the pediatrician and ask for a referral to a speech specialist? Or was Mom right in the fact that Mia did enough talking for the both of them?

She'd had no idea the stress and worry that came with being a mom.

Irelynn's heart broke for the two that were now orphans. She plopped on the couch and pulled her knees to her chest.

Tears pricked her eyes. She couldn't do this. Couldn't raise them on her own. Couldn't keep her promise to Nicole. Couldn't survive financially now that her job was reduced to part-time. Couldn't find another part-time job. Couldn't...

An hour later in bed, sleep eluded her. Irelynn tossed and turned, attempting not to overthink the entire situation. She wanted so desperately to succeed. To make Nicole proud. To be a good mom to the twins.

She did her best to stifle her sobs, lest she wake the children. "Lord, please lead me to another job. I need Your help and Your guidance."

Never will I leave you. Never will I forsake you.

The quiet impressions of the Lord's reassurance pierced her heart. Such an easy thing to believe when life was trouble-free, but not when everything was falling apart.

Irelynn propped up on one elbow. The clock on her nightstand indicated it was 2:57 a.m. If she fell asleep at precisely this moment, she'd have approximately four hours of sleep before Mia and Max awoke.

She took a deep breath. Her mom had been a success story in raising her. It hadn't been easy, and Irelynn remembered the struggles well.

Irelynn, fourteen at the time, had found Mom crying in the kitchen of their dilapidated trailer house. Stacks of bills piled on the counter—the only mess in an otherwise immaculate home with few belongings.

Mom rarely cried. Even when Dad left and never returned, when they purchased a hail-damaged, dented car that limped along on bare tires because it was the only one they could afford, and when they were homeless for two weeks and forced to live in a shelter, Mom never shed a tear. Nor when diagnosed with fibromyalgia did she show any sign of crying.

When they had finally found a trailer to rent that they could afford, word arrived soon after that they might once again be evicted. The factory where Mom worked closed, and with it, 100 employees became unemployed. Mom had hung her head that day, cradling it in her hands, and sobbed.

It was as though everything that could go wrong had gone wrong. The inevitable "last straw." Still, through it all, Mom was Irelynn's hero. Always had been.

Mom had wrapped her arms around Irelynn, and they clung to each other. Until finally, Mom whispered, "God will see us through this. He walks with us, even through the roughest of times."

Irelynn hadn't been so sure that God had even remembered them. Wasn't He like her own father, forgetting she and Mom even existed? "He is faithful. Always faithful," Mom continued, her voice hoarse.

Mom's words repeated over and over in Irelynn's head. *"He is faithful. Always faithful."*

God had been faithful to Mom and Irelynn all those years and through all of those hard times. God would see Irelynn through this. She had to trust He would, for that was the only hope that kept her going.

The tears trickled down her cheeks, this time from the gratitude of knowing the One who was in control.

Everything would be all right. It had to be.

And finally, with the reminder of God's faithfulness, Irelynn fell asleep.

When she awoke two hours later and caught a glimpse of herself in the mirror, she noticed the prominent dark circles under her eyes, the pillow crease on her left cheek, and her hair resembling something of a rat's nest.

Irelynn took a deep breath and clasped her fitness tracker onto her wrist. She heard the twins rustling around on their mattresses in the tight quarters of her room. Within minutes, they jumped onto her bed. Embracing them in a hug, Irelynn did her best to forget about the worries that burdened her and instead focus on the two little lives she had recently become responsible for.

The two children she had grown to love.

The two children she would do anything for.

After some snuggles with Mia and Max, Irelynn helped them get dressed, and then pulled on some athletic leggings and her favorite old oversized t-shirt. No sense in getting dressed up when she wasn't going anywhere today. On the contrary, she needed to do some serious housecleaning and laundry. Who knew that adding two children would increase her laundry load in exponential ways? Who knew they even had so many clothes? Mia, especially, enjoyed changing into several different outfits throughout the day for what she called her "fashion show."

Breakfast, a load of laundry, reading time with the twins, attempts to put them down for a nap while she took a brisk shower, lunch, cleaning the living room and bathroom, coloring pictures with Mia and Max, another load of laundry, snack time... by 3:18 p.m., Irelynn still hadn't had the chance to fix her hair or apply any makeup. She stood in the bathroom, brush in hand, grateful she didn't have any pressing work for today.

Although she desperately needed the work.

The mirror highlighted the dark circles beneath her eyes. She reached for her makeup bag and set it on the bathroom counter. A bit of mascara, eye shadow, and a touch of coverup might at least bring her appearance to acceptable levels. The rat's nest hair persisted, although now at least it was clean. She took the brush to it, bemoaning the fact that she'd inherited her mom's thick coarse hair. If Irelynn could glean just a few more minutes, she would have time to take the flat iron to her hair and tame some of the frizz.

She had just grabbed the flat iron from the shelf when the doorbell rang.

She froze. Who could be visiting at this time of day? Had Quinton mentioned he was coming over to work on the room and she'd forgotten? Was Mrs. Caruthers deciding to pay a visit? If so, the eccentric elderly woman would have plenty to put in her purple notebook after today's encounter with Irelynn.

After a few seconds, the doorbell rang again.

"Someone's at the door," announced Mia. "I think it's Uncle Quinton. Yes, it's Uncle Quinton. Come on, Max."

Uncle Quinton? What was he doing here? Irelynn unplugged the unused flat iron. "Ugh I look like a total wreck," she muttered, and rushed to the door, but not before Mia flung it open.

Sure enough, Quinton stood in the doorway, a smile on his face as he greeted the twins.

Irelynn reached up in an attempt to calm some of the poofiness of her hair. Just a few more minutes and she would have been able to finish the minimal primping to appear halfway presentable.

Yet, now here she stood, looking like a catastrophe.

QUINTON STEPPED up the two stairs to Irelynn's porch and rang the doorbell. He had only two hours to spend today on the remodel so he wanted to get right to it. He could hear noises on the other side of the door, but there was no answer, so he again rang the doorbell.

Mia flung open the door, but Max flew into his arms first. He bear-hugged them and lifted them both off their feet as they giggled. "Aunt Irelynn is a weck."

Quinton set the twins on the floor. "She is?" he asked.

"Yes, a total weck." Mia's blonde curls bobbed with each movement of her small round head.

He chuckled, but when his eyes met Irelynn's it was clear that the fact she was a total "weck" was not amusing to her. "Tell you what? Why don't you two go play for a few minutes while I talk to Aunt Irelynn?"

"Okay," the twins chorused. Max yanked on Mia's arm, which caused her to shriek in response. The two then ran toward the living room.

Irelynn had retreated to the kitchen. He found her there, tackling what appeared to be an oversized load of dishes. "Hey," he said.

"Hi."

"Is everything all right?"

She gave him a strange look. "Why wouldn't it be?"

Quinton took a minute to analyze her appearance. Her normally pretty hair was poufy and sticking out in odd directions like she'd been in a wind storm. Her face appeared tired with bags and circles beneath her eyes. She wore an old worn-out brown t-shirt that sported a hole in the bottom of it and the message, "Coffee isn't only for mornings."

In all the times he'd seen her, she always looked attractive and put-together. Not that he was noticing her looks, because he wasn't.

Okay, so maybe I am.

Or maybe he was just being observant, for which Nicole would be proud. She'd always retorted that he was unobservant.

Irelynn stood facing him, hands on her hips, awaiting his answer. What was the question? *Oh, yeah.* "You just look..."

"Yes?"

"Uh..."

"Terrible?"

She could never look terrible. As a matter of fact, she still looked *somewhat* pretty even with her strange hairdo and tired eyes. "I didn't say that."

Her expression told him he didn't have to say words for her to get the gist of his thoughts. "You just don't look like yourself is all." He paused. "So...are you all right? Is it the twins?"

Irelynn shook her head far too hastily. "No, not the twins at all."

"Is it your mom?"

"No, she's fine."

"Good to hear." This conversation was clearly getting them nowhere. "Is it Mrs. Caruthers?"

Irelynn shot him a shocked expression. "Mrs. Caruthers? Why would it be her?"

"I don't know. She just came to mind, you know, with her nosy notetaking and all that."

A slight grin lit her face, and he realized he actually liked it when she smiled. And when she blushed. That was cute too.

Whoa. Not even going there. Obviously, the hectic work week had messed with his brain cells.

"No, it's not Mrs. Caruthers." She paused. "Quinton, why are you asking me all these questions? It's not like we're friends."

A shred of disappointment took root in Quinton's gut. What if they were friends? Wouldn't that make life easier for the twins? For keeping Nicole's promise? Maybe convenient, but highly unlikely. "You're right, we're not." He shrugged. "I guess I was just wondering, you know, with your hair and stuff."

Irelynn narrowed her eyes at him, and Quinton knew he'd said the wrong words. Typical. For some reason, he was more than adept at choosing the wrong words when talking with her.

"The hair?"

"You know. It's kind of..."

"Yes?"

Ugh. Back to the appearance thing again. Hadn't they hashed this over at the beginning of their awkward conversation? "It's just, uh, a different style."

"Because you are the hairdo expert?"

Quinton chuckled. "No, not exactly." Why were women such a

mystery, anyway? Men just laid it all out in the forefront when something was wrong. Solved the problem and got it done and over with. Women, on the other hand, were puzzles that no man wanted to get caught trying to solve. Especially not him. Especially not with Irelynn.

Except that he wanted to solve this puzzle. Why was beyond him.

A squawk of disagreement from the twins interrupted their exchange. "How have they been today?"

"Good."

Back to the one-word answers. This was getting him nowhere. He checked his fitness tracker. Exactly one hour and forty-five minutes to do the stuff he needed to do before he left to meet with the plumber at one of the houses in Waterbury Acres.

"Glad to hear everything is all right then."

Even if he could explain it, he couldn't. If that even made sense. But he did care. Cared for her. Cared what happened in her life. He wouldn't tell her that, though.

"It was just a long night."

"Yeah. I've had those."

The silence that followed was awkward, and he wondered what else to say. She turned from him and busied herself at the kitchen sink. Her shoulders drooped, as if she bore a hefty burden.

Something in his heart twisted.

Before Quinton could stop himself or even think rationally about what he was doing, he reached a hand toward her arm. They were cemented together for the next 15 years in the challenge of raising Mia and Max. Even if her disposition today had nothing to do with the twins, Quinton was sure all the changes hadn't been easy for her either.

The realization caught him off guard.

Quinton's hand rested on her arm, which was cool to the touch. He leaned toward her and attempted to be in her line of vision. Her green eyes glistened and he hoped those weren't masked tears hidden in their depths.

"Why do you care, Quinton?" she whispered. Not sarcastically, not rudely. Just a matter-of-fact question.

"I don't know. I just...you're Nicole's friend, and she would want to know what's wrong."

Except that he wasn't Nicole. Wasn't her best friend. Wasn't someone with whom she could or would confide. They weren't even friends, more like distant acquaintances with a dislike for each other.

So why then...?

Distrust lined her features. Irelynn set the bowl down in the sink and her chin trembled. He hoped she wouldn't cry. Quinton, for sure, didn't know what to do about tears.

Besides, what did enemies do when one of them was upset, not due to the other's fault? Or maybe it was his fault she was upset. *Man, talk about clueless.*

"Is it me?"

She let out a half-laugh and faced him again. "Well, we are nemeses."

"Nemeses?" He hadn't heard that word since his junior year in high school on the end-of-the-year vocabulary test.

"But no, it's not you."

Why that relieved him, he didn't know. Realizing his hand was still resting on her arm, he should probably remove it, but she seemed comforted by it. Or maybe it was just his imagination. After wrestling with himself for a half a minute, he decided to leave it there, resisting the urge to...

Do what? Pull her into a friendly hug? Sit down with her and talk about what bothered her? He was a clueless guy for crying out loud.

What would Nicole want him to do about the sadness that plagued her best friend?

Quinton cleared his throat. "I've been thinking of taking the kids to that new pizza joint with all the fun games that just opened on Morton Avenue. How about we all go there tonight?"

"The kids would love to go there, I'm sure. But you can take them, I can stay home."

"No, I meant you can go too." A tear in her green eyes made them sparkle.

Get a grip, Quinton. You don't need to be noticing her eyes. This is Irelynn Brady. Or did you forget?

The words he needed to say for her—the words Nicole would want him to say—stuck in his throat and croaked out as he uttered them. "I...Nicole...would want you to go."

Irelynn's expression caused him concern that she had misinterpreted his words. He needed to clear that up and fast. "I mean, I know that pizza generally solves all life's problems. It does for me, anyway. A thick crust pepperoni pizza with extra cheese has a way of making all right with the world again."

A slight smile formed on her face. He was making progress. Nicole would be proud.

"Besides. My mom always said that one of the best things you can do for a woman is relieve her of the task of making dinner when it's been a hard day."

"Your mom was a wise woman."

"See there? We do have something we agree on." Quinton offered her a smile, hoping she'd offer one in return.

She didn't disappoint him. A full smile filled her face. *Man, is she pretty, or what? No, she is not. She's Irelynn. Nicole's best friend. Joint guardian of the twins. An irritating, snobby woman who makes life more difficult. But she is sort of pretty and she cares about the kids and all. She has to. That's what Nicole wanted her to do.* Quinton blinked. What sane man argued with himself this way in his mind? Maybe he was the one who needed the pizza break. "I know women would prefer shopping or something, but you know, men, they solve problems with pizza all the time. It's been passed down from generation to generation."

"Is that so?"

"It is."

Irelynn appeared to be lightening up a bit. Maybe all of this hard work was paying off. She looked down at his hand on her arm.

And Quinton instantly removed it. Odd. He missed having his hand there offering her comfort. He sure wasn't going to admit that to anyone or even himself. Besides, all of this Mr. Cheer-up was for Nicole.

"It would take me a few minutes to get ready, so why don't you guys just go ahead."

"I have to fix something in the room, and then I have to run over to one of the houses I'm working on in the Waterbury Acres Subdivision. It'll be a couple hours before we go. Closer to dinner time."

"Oh. Okay."

Or maybe she'd like to see the house in Waterbury Acres. It was coming along nicely. Should he ask her? "Or you could get ready and we could all go over to the house and then head directly to the pizza place."

Why would he want her to go to the new house? Why would *she* care to go?

Irelynn appeared to ponder his suggestion, just about the time he wished he could retract it. "That might work. I've heard that subdivision is really growing."

"It is. Back when I was a kid, it was just farmland. The developer has done a remarkable job with it."

"I can try to get myself and the kids ready in the time you're here checking out whatever you need to do in the room."

Quinton nodded. Was it too soon for victory? Nicole would be offering him kudos right about now. "All right, then. I'll go do what I need to do, and then we'll go."

Irelynn offered him another smile. Yep, victory. Nicole would be proud.

Strange.

Quinton acted like he actually cared. And then to suggest pizza?

And Irelynn had agreed.

Apparently, she was more exhausted than she thought.

Quinton's warm hand on her arm oddly provided a measure of comfort. And sent tingles racing from her forearm all the way to her shoulder.

Craziness.

When he removed his hand all too soon, she wished again for the warmth and comfort it provided.

As soon as the thought entered her mind, Irelynn dismissed it. One thing was certain...she needed to clean up a bit—or a lot—before going with the twins and Quinton to the pizza place.

The burdens of her job cut, money woes, and pressure to be the kind of mom Nicole would have wanted her to be temporarily eased. Maybe Quinton was right. Maybe pizza, or the mere thought of it, did fix everything.

Had he actually been concerned about her? Was it genuine?

Not like she could tell him what was truly bothering her. If she did, Quinton would think her unable to raise the children.

Him seeing her looking like a "weck," as Mia would say, had been nothing short of an embarrassment. But Irelynn didn't care about what he thought about her appearance. Right?

After making sure the children were dressed and Mia's hair fixed, Irelynn ran to her room and did her best to fix her appearance, which still resembled someone who had been run over by a huge moving truck. She finished brushing her hair, pulled it into a ponytail, washed her face, and applied some fresh makeup. The circles under her eyes remained, but her overall countenance improved. Next, she pulled on some jeans, a flattering button-up long-sleeved spring plaid top, and her brown boots.

Nicole would have been proud of her for accepting the offer to accompany Quinton and the twins to dinner. She wouldn't even bring up the fact that last time they were to have dinner resulted in a no-show, a rude action on his part.

So maybe Quinton was only 95 percent her nemesis instead of 99 percent.

CHAPTER 10

The ride to see the Waterbury Acres home was made mostly in silence until they reached the entrance to the new subdivision. "This place sure has changed since I was a kid," Quinton commented.

Irelynn gazed out the window. A sizeable arc across the road indicated they had arrived at the subdivision. Smooth river rock detailed the pillars that held up the arc. New trees lined either side as they drove along the paved road. Houses worth more than six or seven times that of Irelynn's dotted the green expanses of lawn. Some were completely done and obviously resided in, while others were in various stages of construction.

"The developer has done an incredible job with the infrastructure. He's put in walkways and they have some of the fastest internet speeds in the county. It's far out of my price range, but it's pretty cool to be able to build a couple of homes here."

Far out anyone's price range, Irelynn thought. The houses were mammoth with expansive windows, covered porches, and detailed rock work. "It reminds me of a golf course community in the city I grew up in," she said. Mom cleaned homes for the wealthy folks living near the golf course when Irelynn was in elementary school.

Quinton pulled into the driveway of a contemporary farm-house. A massive wraparound porch, pointed roof design, and a classy choice of windows greeted her. "It's about 4,000 square feet," he said, helping Max from the backseat.

Irelynn was impressed by the outside, but even more so by the inside of the in-process home. A rock fireplace lined the wall of the living room. Wood flooring and stainless steel appliances, including an upper end stove, filled the kitchen. She walked toward the stove. "This could be in a restaurant."

She could only imagine the baking she could do with an oven like that.

"The entire kitchen could be in a restaurant. The wife wanted something decent-sized so she could entertain. I think I could fit at least three of my kitchen and dining rooms in just the kitchen area of this house."

Irelynn took in the vaulted ceilings. The kitchen was as big as her entire house.

"Come on, I'll give you a tour."

Quinton led her and the children on a tour of first the down-stairs, then the upstairs of the spacious home. He excused himself to speak to the plumber, who had just arrived, before meeting her on the back deck. "The view is insane," he said.

Irelynn took in the view of the distant mountains. What would it be like to live in such a place? Suddenly, her home seemed more like a tent than an actual wood dwelling. "This is impressive," she said.

"I learned from the best. My dad was amazing when it came to construction. But it's not only that, it's all the coordinating of sub-contractors. He excelled at that." He paused. "Are you kids ready to go get some pizza?"

"Pizza!" the two chorused.

Irelynn followed Quinton to the truck. Was there was more to Quinton Gregory than met the eye?

THE LOW HUM of the Christian radio station played in an otherwise quiet vehicle during the ride to the pizza restaurant. The twins had fallen asleep in the backseat, and Quinton seemed to be in deep thought.

Irelynn cast a glance at her somewhat-of-a-nemesis. She was impressed by his construction skills and the dedication and discipline it took to run a business. The fact that Quinton could build an entire house, and not just any house, but a custom home, gave him more credibility, especially when it came to her simple remodel job.

Quinton.

She had to give the man credit. He not only was providing a meal for them so she could save what she'd planned for dinner for another day, but he had also succeeded in helping her take her mind off her current situation. While it wasn't the diversion Irelynn would have chosen, nonetheless the problems of last night seemed more manageable.

The overwhelmed feelings of trying to deal with the job cut, putting food on the table, parenting the twins, and missing Nicole were still there, but the Lord had reminded her once again that He would walk with her through the entire ordeal.

And He had used an unexpected person to achieve it.

Still, while Quinton had lightened her load, at least for today, Irelynn couldn't share with him the real reasons for her distress. For doing so could cause him to believe she wasn't able to care for the kids.

And she would allow nothing to jeopardize her dedication to Nicole and the promise she'd made.

Nothing.

QUINTON STOLE a quick glance at Irelynn. While quiet, she did seem to at least be in a more lighthearted mood than earlier. Perhaps his suggestion to see the new house, followed by pizza at The Pizza Slice, had made a positive impact on her.

And Irelynn had mentioned the house he was building was impressive. Something about her comment kept replaying over and over in his mind. That Irelynn would be impressed by anything to do with him was nothing short of a miracle. Her opinion of him mattered for some reason, even if it was only her opinion of his construction abilities. If Quinton could convince her that he really wasn't so bad, maybe they could get along better for the children's sake. And for Nicole.

Showing Irelynn that he could provide for Mia and Max was critical. He couldn't have her thinking otherwise. Showing her that he had it all together and was succeeding at successfully running his business proved Nicole had made the right choice. Not that she wouldn't have chosen Quinton for the task, but a man had to be able to provide for his family.

And Quinton could do that.

He might fail at other aspects of raising the children, like feeding them enough vegetables, but he'd always provide for them.

Even if the plumber was causing some havoc and taking far longer than necessary to get the job done that he was hired to do. Hopefully Quinton's brief discussion with him at the house moments ago would encourage the man to get his priorities in order.

A check in his rearview mirror indicated Mia and Max had taken a nap. Irelynn's arm rested on the console between them. Why did he have a strange urge to take her hand in his and reassure her that they could do this? That they could not only accomplish what Nicole had asked of them, but could actually do it well?

Take her hand in his?

Whoa.

So not happening. He had probably already sent her the wrong message this morning when he'd consoled her.

Quinton sighed. Irelynn loved the twins. Nicole had known what she was doing when she had assigned Irelynn the task of co-raising Mia and Max. Not that Quinton would admit that to Irelynn or anyone else. And she did love the Lord. That was important. And she was pretty.

And...

She irritated him. More than any other person who had ever lived. And she had stood him up at Fernandez's Restaurant.

So why was Irelynn on his mind more than usual today?

IRELYNN HADN'T YET BEEN to The Pizza Slice restaurant. Mia and Max could apparently tell this wasn't the usual type of restaurant from the moment they emerged from the truck and heard the carnival-like music. Mia tugged on Irelynn's hand and pointed in the direction of the restaurant. "Can we go to that place?"

The enthusiasm lighting Mia's face did wonders for Irelynn's demeanor. "Yes, we can."

Max, holding on to Quinton's hand, did a jig with his short legs and hastened Quinton to walk faster.

"I think the kids are excited to go here," Quinton said.

Irelynn nodded. Maybe coming wasn't such a bad idea after all.

The atmosphere inside the pizza place catered to children, which was evident by the decorations, the music, and the multitude of games and activities.

The teenage waitress with pink highlights in her hair led them to a booth against the far wall. "Here's the menu," she said, smacking her gum. "I'll be back in a few minutes to take your order."

Quinton grabbed two booster seats from the towering pile and slid one onto each side of the booth.

"Can we wide on that?" Max asked, his eyes round as he pointed to the jacked-up toy truck.

"Don't let Max drive!" exclaimed Mia with a giggle.

Irelynn's eyes connected with Quinton's and they both laughed. "Tell me we have awhile before they get their driver's licenses," quipped Quinton.

"I don't even want to think about that or the teenage years. Suddenly age three seems really easy."

"That's the truth."

He held her gaze for a minute until Irelynn looked away, feeling the blush creep up her cheeks. Would they survive long enough without killing each other to see the twins emerge into the formidable teenage years?

With Quinton being 95 percent her nemesis, the odds weren't in their favor.

Or maybe 94 percent after his kindness this afternoon.

Irelynn watched as Quinton swung first Max into the driver's seat, then Mia beside him. Max immediately placed one hand on the wheel and slouched. "Want the wadio?"

"All right, where did he learn that?" Irelynn asked, noting Max's cocky disposition as he "drove" the truck.

"No idea."

Irelynn laughed at Quinton's comment, surprising herself that she found him to have an enjoyable sense of humor. Perhaps she was just delirious from all the stress.

"Please take me shopping," demanded Mia, clasping Baby in her arms.

"Now where did she learn that?" Quinton tossed Irelynn a look that told her he already knew the answer.

"No idea."

They shared a look between them, and Irelynn held her breath. Much more of this camaraderie and she might end up reducing Quinton's nemesis factor to 90 percent.

Moments later after the twins had tired of the truck, Quinton nodded toward a corner of the room. "I challenge you to a round of air hockey."

Challenge her? Oh, she'd love to challenge him. It'd be even better if she won that challenge. "I might be slightly competitive when it comes to air hockey. Just warning you."

"No worries with that. I'm the same way. Air hockey is one of my favorite games."

"I'm not going to ruin the evening and let you know that that means we have something in common."

Quinton laughed, not a bad laugh for a somewhat-of-a-nemesis. Actually, kind of a nice laugh, but Irelynn hadn't had much sleep last night, so surely such a thought only stemmed from pure exhaustion.

"Mia and Max, why don't you be our cheerleaders?" She dragged two chairs to the side of the air hockey table.

"What's a deerleader?"

Quinton lifted Mia and placed her on one chair and Max on the other. "A cheerleader is someone who tries to get their team to win by saying 'go, go.' You say that to Aunt Irelynn and me as we try to win each other."

"Okay. Max and me will be deerleaders. Can Aunt Irelynn win?"

Irelynn did her best to stifle a prideful giggle when Quinton caught her eye. "Seems there's some favoritism going on here," he whispered.

Oh, but that I could win Quinton at this one thing. Perhaps I could forget the burdens of everyday life if I could have victory at air hockey against my biggest rival.

Irelynn stood at one end of the 42" table, while Quinton stood at the other. With mallet in hand, she prepared to win.

"Just to warn you, no one wins 'The Quinton' when it comes to air hockey. I was the champion among my friends in high school."

"Your friends weren't real competition."

Quinton chuckled. "Maybe not, but we had a lot of practice on the old air hockey table in my room growing up."

"I'm no slouch myself. We lived near an arcade at one point when I was in junior high. Have you heard the term 'a force to be reckoned with?'"

"You don't intimidate me one bit."

Of course not. Nothing can intimate Mr. Arrogance.

Irelynn hit the puck across the table. Nicole would be so proud of them for getting along, even if it meant a fierce challenge of air hockey. Quinton blocked the puck and sent it back over to her side. She narrowly stopped him from scoring.

"Told you I was a professional," he bragged.

"'Pride comes before a fall," Irelynn quipped, causing the puck to slam into the goal box. "One point for Irelynn."

Mia cheered. "Go, Aunt Irelynn. Is that what I'm posed ta say?"

"Yes."

"No."

Irelynn thought of the irony that they were disagreeing even about how Mia was to cheer. She took a hurried glance at the children. Mia continued to cheer while Max clapped his hands and grinned the cutest little boy smile Irelynn had ever seen.

She loved those two more than she'd ever thought possible.

Maybe God really would get her through all of this.

"All right, now that we're warmed up, no more charity," said Quinton, bringing her back to the moment.

Wasn't he the cocky one? Irelynn focused on the game, pushing aside some of the burdens that weighed heavily on her heart. What better way to prove a point than to win your most vehement opponent?

The close game continued. "We're tied," Irelynn commented, sending the puck back across the line. Soon, a couple other families had lined up to watch the game.

"Not for long." Quinton sent the puck skidding across the table, making another goal.

"Wow, honey, we need to play a game of air hockey. I hear activities like this are recommended for maintaining a healthy marriage," said a woman spectator to her husband.

"Oh, we're not..." Irelynn began, her focus interrupted as Quinton scored another goal on her.

"I'm two ahead now." Was it Irelynn's imagination or had Quinton just puffed out his muscular chest?

But who was noticing whether he was muscular or scrawny?

Certainly not her.

With finesse and strategy, Irelynn sent the puck into the goal. "Now you're one ahead. We're narrowing it down."

"Can we place bets on who wins?" asked another spectator.

Irelynn did her best not to let the crowd distract her. An introvert's nightmare, for sure, with all these people clustering around to watch her and Quinton. Making sure that Mia and Max were still behaving, she leaned to one side and made yet another goal. "Tied game, once again."

Quinton sent the puck over, and Irelynn barely blocked it before sending it back.

At just that time, the waitress came around the corner. "Your pizza is ready."

Glancing up just briefly to see the oversized pepperoni pizza was Quinton's downfall. Irelynn scored on him. "Game won."

The enthusiastic crowd that had gathered cheered. "We should have placed bets," Irelynn overhead someone say.

"Hey, wait. We're not done." Quinton maintained his stance at the end of the air hockey table. But it was too late. Irelynn already assisted Mia and Max from the chairs and toward the table.

"I'll try not to gloat that I annihilated 'The Quinton,'" Irelynn said, rolling her eyes.

"My mom always taught me to let a girl win so it doesn't hurt her feelings. Besides, being a gentleman is important to me."

"Right. Excuses, excuses."

Quinton feigned a hurt expression. "You don't believe me?"

"Not in the least."

"Hey, at least let's agree to have a rematch. Maybe I was slightly rusty since high school."

A rematch? So not happening...or well, maybe it would be fun. Not that I'll ever admit that to you, Mr. Arrogance. "Maybe," she said, instead choosing to be evasive.

"I gonna sit next to Max." Mia took one booster seat from the opposite side of the table and plopped the two orange booster chairs next to each other on one side of the booth.

Irelynn was about to suggest they sit on opposite sides when Quinton gestured for her to slide into the empty side of the booth. Was everyone all right with this seating arrangement except her? Maybe she could talk Quinton into sitting on the opposite side with one of the children. "Are you sure you want to sit by the winner?"

"I don't want to at all, but if it keeps things from becoming a Sutherland's Fine Dining episode, I'll make the sacrifice." He slid in next to her.

He did have a point, but this was awkward.

His shoulder rubbed hers for the briefest of moments. And why should that have any impact on her?

It doesn't, Irelynn convinced herself.

Quinton blessed the meal, then divvied out the pizza slices. "Please cut mine?" Mia slid her plate toward Irelynn. In reaching for it, her arm collided with Quinton's. A peculiar tingle zipped up her arm.

"Pizza is a finger food," said Quinton, taking a bite.

"She's always liked to have it cut up. She's a classy dame," laughed Irelynn, trying to take her mind off the fact that she truly did not like sitting so close to Quinton.

"Feed me?"

Irelynn put the first bite of pizza on a fork and fed it to Mia.

"She also likes to be fed the first bite after I cut up her food." She noticed a look she couldn't define lining Quinton's expression.

Quickly, so as to avoid staring, Irelynn returned her gaze to her pizza.

"I'm a baby birdy," quipped Mia in a voice much younger and exaggerated than her own. "Ahhhh..." she opened her mouth wide to receive another bite. "Just like baby birdies when their mama feeds them."

Irelynn placed another bite in Mia's mouth. "We love reading a book called *'Baby Bird'* at home."

Max nodded. "Baby bird," he repeated.

Again, Irelynn felt Quinton's gaze upon her. She turned her head, their faces just inches from each other. Some strange sensation zinged through her stomach. Hunger pains, perhaps?

Time stopped for a moment and Irelynn held her breath. This close, the man was even more attractive.

Irelynn looked away. She for sure had to get more sleep tonight or she'd be certifiably insane.

After eating and the twins spending time playing more games, they loaded up in the truck and started toward Irelynn's house. "See why a large pepperoni pizza always makes things better?"

Irelynn was about to say she agreed since pepperoni pizza with extra cheese was her favorite comfort food too, but she bit her tongue. She would not...absolutely would not...have something else in common with the frustrating Quinton Gregory.

And why did he seem a little less frustrating tonight?

She dared not even contemplate the answer.

SILENCE FILLED the air during the ride to Irelynn's house, giving Quinton time to contemplate the evening. He didn't want to admit it, but he'd actually enjoyed his time with Irelynn, especially during their air hockey match.

Even though he'd lost.

Then sitting next to her at the table. He took his mind off the close proximity next to her and instead focused on the *truth* of the matter. Nicole would be proud of them for not arguing much tonight and for making the best of the situation for the twins.

And even though Quinton may not want to admit it, Irelynn was the perfect choice as a mom to Mia and Max. She'd earned his respect for cutting up Mia's food and playing her "baby bird" game with her. Nicole had been correct in choosing Irelynn to be a part of Mia's and Max's lives.

Even if they weren't friends.

Still, hopefully his attempt at cheering her up from whatever was bothering her earlier had been effective. Nicole would have wanted it that way.

The children had fallen asleep in the truck on the way home, and Quinton offered to carry one, then the other to their beds. When he finished, he walked to the porch. Irelynn followed him.

"Thank you for taking us out to pizza," she said.

"Sure."

"Even if I did annihilate you in our game of air hockey." Her green eyes twinkled in the soft glow of the porch light. Not that he noticed such things.

"Not sure I'd call it an annihilation. As I recall, it was a close game, tied until the waitress told us it was time for pizza. It was a hard call for me...dodge directly over for the first slice of pizza or defeat you in air hockey."

"Oh, really. If I recall, it was that someone has actually unseated the air hockey champion famously known as 'The Quinton' for no other reason that she is simply a better player."

Bantering back and forth with Irelynn was fun. Who would have thought? Maybe they could get along after all, and maybe even be friends for the children, of course. And Nicole.

Quinton heard the sound of a door, and glanced over to see Mrs. Caruthers popping her head out of her door in their direction. She jotted something in her notebook, then stepped back inside her house. "Seems we have a spy in the neighborhood."

"One of these days I'm going to bribe her with a dozen home-made cookies just so I can see what's inside that notebook of hers."

"Probably notes on the mail carrier and on every single person in the neighborhood."

They stood there then, in silence. Irelynn folded her arms across her chest, and he wondered if she was cold in the crisp night air.

"I should go."

"Yes."

Yet, neither of them moved. His feet remained planted on the wooden porch. In the distance, a dog barked. Mrs. Caruthers's light flicked off. The smell of rain permeated the air.

He cleared his throat. "Good night, Irelynn."

"Good night, Quinton."

With that, he finally willed his feet to carry him to his truck.

CHAPTER 11

Irelynn had finally secured a website-building assignment outside of her normal job. The Lord was truly watching out for her. She hadn't yet heard back on either of the two part-time jobs she recently applied for, but Mom insisted it took time for employers to reach out to potential employees, especially if there were more people to interview.

Even so, Irelynn refused to give up hope. Things were looking up. While the twins took their nap, she situated herself at her office desk and began building the website for Kylie's Critters, the new pet shop in town. Perhaps someday Irelynn's dream of having her own company building websites for businesses would come to fruition. Until then, she'd continue working for Jamie and doing some websites on the side. And hopefully land another part-time job.

Quinton returned from lunch. "Hey, Irelynn," he said, as he passed through the living room. She never really noticed his smile before, but she had to admit that even those who fell into the category of somewhat-of-a-nemesis could have handsome smiles.

Besides, she and Quinton had gotten along a lot better since their pizza outing and the fun they had playing air hockey. Something had changed between them. It was as though they were both doing their best attempt to be somewhat on the same side. The side that desired to raise Mia and Max as Nicole had wished. And Quinton's nemesis factor had dropped to the high 80s.

She might even consider forgiving him for standing her up at Fernando's.

"Hi, Quinton."

"Hey. Are the kids down for a nap?"

"Yes. Finally."

"I have some things to work on in their rooms, but it shouldn't be too loud."

"Thank you. I'm working on a new website, so I'll take whatever time I can get." She offered a smile of her own. Their eyes connected. Neither looked away. Something fluttered in her stomach and she willed herself not to blush.

How could someone she didn't really care much for have such an effect on her?

And why was she even pondering it?

Irelynn was the first to look away. "Well, I better let you get to work."

"You too."

But he didn't move. "Irelynn?"

"Yes?"

"That was fun at the pizza place the other night."

"It was. Thank you for taking my mind off things."

Quinton chuckled a low-rumbling laugh, one Irelynn was becoming accustomed to. "Pizza has a way of making things better. We often thank the Lord for the big things, but when was the last time we thanked Him for pizza?"

"We don't thank Him nearly enough for it."

Their locked gaze returned. Irelynn did blush then, and she chastised herself. Surely he saw it, and she doubted he would believe she had suddenly developed a sunburn. Irelynn focused her attention on her computer screen, then back to him.

He was still watching her. Irelynn shifted in her chair and averted her eyes back to the screen. If this continued, Kylie's Critters would never have a new website.

To his credit, Quinton changed the subject. "I saw you running the other day."

"Oh?"

"Mind if I join you sometime?"

"I didn't know you ran. Oh wait, I guess I do remember Carlos saying something about running track with you in high school."

Quinton leaned against the wall. "I'm impressed that you remember."

The blush crept up her cheeks all over again. Drat her light complexion. *Thanks, Dutch ancestry.* And the continual blush? Why not just resign herself to the fact that she'd forever be a cherry face instead of being able to mask her emotions?

Wait—emotions?

Quinton awaited her answer. Mulling over complexions and emotions would have to wait. "I didn't really remember, it's just that..." *Just that what?*

"Anyway, I'd like to join you sometime. I'll even push the stroller."

Irelynn swallowed hard, willing, begging, *praying* her face would return to its normal shade. "What a deal," she muttered, her voice sounding shaky.

Good grief. Why was he having this effect on her? Did she forget he was Quinton Gregory? A momentary lapse in judgment?

The snarky comment had slipped out before Irelynn could stop it, and Quinton appeared offended. "I just thought it would be fun. The close proximity to the pathways from this neighborhood is so convenient."

"Yes. Yes, it is. I didn't mean to sound rude. Sure, you can join us sometime."

"Thanks. I'll take you up on that." He patted his stomach. "I need to start running again. Need to watch the pounds, you know?"

Watch the pounds? Irelynn rolled her eyes. The guy probably had six-pack abs. Try being a sudden mom with a crazy hectic schedule and an affection for cheese crackers. Then talk about needing to watch pounds.

And just why am I even noticing Quinton's physique? Totally not enough sleep last night.

There was an uncomfortable silence then, and Irelynn did her best to focus on the website building. Somewhat difficult with her nemesis looking over her shoulder.

Her fingers fumbled on the keys and typed all kinds of strange letters, not even doable for the coding of the website. More like some foreign language. She hit the backspace button and turned her head around to see him watching her. Irelynn spun in her chair and faced him again.

"Look, Irelynn..."

For some odd reason, Irelynn held her breath. What was he about to say?

"I was looking at that house down the block for sale. You know, the one at 1446 Whitmore Street?"

An image of the dilapidated house on the next block entered her mind. "Yes?"

"I'm looking at it."

Did Quinton want to purchase it for himself? Surely not. Surely, he was wanting to buy it as a fixer-upper and turn around and flip it. He had a knack for remodeling, not that she would have admitted that a week ago. "That's a substantial project to fix up and sell, but I think it's a fantastic idea. It would sure improve the neighborhood."

Quinton shook his head. "No, not to fix up and sell. To live there."

All right. So the guy had some admirable qualities. Loved God, loved his country, devoted uncle, talented carpenter, good-looking even, but she so did not want him living down the street. She'd never get away from him then. "You would want to live there? I thought it was condemned."

"Not yet, but it should be. The person who used to live there really trashed the place. But, yeah, I'd like to live there with the twins." He shrugged his broad shoulders. *Broad shoulders? Get a grip, Irelynn.*

"Why would you want to live there?"

"Nice neighborhood, close to the jogging paths and the park, and ease of picking up the kids and dropping them off at your house. My apartment isn't big enough for the three of us."

"But it's so…"

"I know, right? While the house is pretty beat up inside, it does have some potential. The backyard could be nice with minimal work. I'm still crunching numbers to see if it's something I can take on." He paused and narrowed his eyes at her. "Is it a problem if I live down the road? It's not like it's next door or across the street."

"I…uh…" she'd never stuttered in her life. Not really. Not unless you count the time the teacher in seventh grade asked where her homework was and Irelynn used the flimsy excuse that the dog had eaten it, knowing the teacher would never believe her, especially since she'd never owned a dog.

Quinton appeared to be waiting. How could she tell the truth and not be unkind? "It's just that you and me—we aren't exactly friends."

"We aren't?"

Was he kidding? Irelynn knew he didn't like her any more than she liked him. Although, the "friend meter" had increased a tiny bit since the pizza night. Not enough to be consequential, however. She looked up at him. Teasing lit his blue eyes. "No, we really aren't," she squeaked.

Some kind of expression flashed through those eyes. Disappointment, perhaps? But no, he wouldn't be disappointed that they weren't friends.

"Anyway, I'm going to be looking at the house again to see if there's too much work to do to get it up to a livable standard. Cosmetic stuff I can work on later, but the place needs some serious electric and plumbing help, not to mention a thorough cleaning. And it's only if I can get it for a steal, so no need to worry yet."

Irelynn let out the breath she'd been holding. It wouldn't work to have him down the block. Too close. She'd have to see him too often then.

But is that really a bad thing?

Well, it isn't a good thing, so hush, inner voice.

Fantastic. She was talking to herself and answering. "I noticed there's a house over on Primrose for sale. A nice two-story one."

"Really, Irelynn, you're not the best at hinting without being obvious."

"Sorry, it's just that, it probably wouldn't work for us to be living so close to each other. And besides, what would Mrs. Caruthers say?"

"She'd jot it all down in her notebook—our comings and goings. She'd have her binoculars out so she could see clear down to the next block, past the other houses, past the trees..."

"True."

"Speaking of Mrs. Caruthers, maybe she'd be willing to sell me her house. Then I really could be next door. Think of how convenient that would be."

Irelynn saw the twinkle in Quinton's eyes and knew he was again teasing her.

She found she liked that subtle hint of giving each other a hard time.

"Well..." Irelynn began. "I don't know if she'd go for it. You see, she has some prime real estate when it comes to spying on the neighborhood. Perhaps for a high price, she might consider it."

Quinton grinned. "Then again, if you're concerned about me being a block away, it's never going work having me next door."

"I agree. But as they say, you can choose your friends, but you can't choose your neighbors."

"That's true." Quinton appeared to be thinking for a moment. "The house down the block might not work out anyway. And for the record, the house on Primrose is way out of my price range. Look, I'd better get to work and let you get to work before the twins wake up."

For some reason after their conversation, Irelynn couldn't keep her mind on the new website.

Quinton Gregory was so not a good influence on her.

CHAPTER 12

Quinton attempted to keep his mind on the task of the remodel, to no avail. The conversation with Irelynn was mixed: sometimes he thought maybe she could consider a friendship with him. Other times, like the whole house issue made him realize she liked him about as much as he liked her.

And true to what she said, they weren't friends. Not like he wanted to be friends.

Although shouldn't they be? For Nicole?

Then there was the whole blushing thing. It was cute the way her face turned red whenever he joked around with her.

Yes, he did admire Irelynn. Her mothering of Mia and Max, her obvious concern and compassion for others, and her ability to make a website from nothing. If she wasn't so difficult...

The whole house thing bothered him. Was it really smart to live so close? The convenience would be handy, and he had no doubt he could give the house a complete makeover. But to live just down the street?

The Primrose Street house she'd mentioned was so far beyond his budget, it was comical. Should he more heavily consider the other house on Fourth Street?

Whatever house he decided to purchase, his main motivation was to care for the kids and raise them as if they were his own. Although, if he was unable to keep his promise of keeping Tom safe during their deployment, what made Quinton think he could effectively care for Mia and Max?

Gram and the twins were the only family he had left. He would endeavor to succeed in the role of raising them, no matter what the future held.

Failure in this matter wasn't an option.

QUINTON HAD PRAYED a lot about this house. He'd spoken to Gram about it and sought her advice. He bounced the idea off his men's group Bible study leader. It just seemed so convenient, and if he could negotiate a lower price, he might be able to afford all the rehabilitation the house required.

After another prayer for guidance, Quinton made a phone call. "Isabelle Vacura, how may I help you with your real estate needs?" Her high-pitched voice chirped on the other end.

"Isabelle, hey, this is Quinton Gregory. I was wondering if I could make an appointment to look at that house again."

"Sure, what's your schedule like?"

He gave her some possible dates and times, and they settled on the following afternoon. It would fit his schedule to look at the house, then go directly to pick up Mia and Max for his time with them over the weekend.

It still bothered him, however, that Irelynn wasn't keen on his idea to live a block away. Not that he needed her permission. He would like her to be somewhat in agreeance, however. If for nothing else, for the ease of transferring the kids. Especially as they got older, it would make it a lot easier than driving the several miles one way to retrieve and return them. Christmas, birthdays, and all the other holidays would be a lot easier too.

No, Quinton didn't figure he and Irelynn to be friends. Hesitant acquaintances at the most. Although, he thought maybe their time spent at The Pizza Slice had changed things for the better. Maybe it had been his imagination. But one thing was for sure. He'd never take an interest in her.

Not even for Nicole.

When 2:00 p.m. the following day arrived, Quinton drove his truck to meet Isabelle at the house. As he parked on the side of the road in front of the house, a thought occurred to him. Maybe he ought to ask Irelynn to come take a look at the house too. Perhaps she was hesitant because she was concerned about the twins being raised in a building that should be condemned. He needed to reiterate to her that he wouldn't be allowing the twins to live there until he'd made sure the house was structurally sound, thoroughly cleaned, including making sure there were no mold issues, and had updated plumbing and electric.

And maybe, just maybe, by that time, they would get along better. Maybe even like each other as friends.

For Nicole and the twins, of course.

He thoroughly inspected what he could of the exterior until he saw a familiar black SUV.

"Hello, Quinty." Isabelle rushed toward him, her walk exaggerated due to her high-heeled sandals. How had she not twisted an ankle? She sidled up alongside him and gently squeezed his upper arm. "How are you today?"

"Doing good. I want to look through the house again and take some notes."

"Of course." She unlocked the lockbox and led the way through the house. In the short time since he'd last seen it, Quinton had forgotten just how dilapidated it was. He'd made up his mind that if his offer, or an amount close to it, wasn't accepted, this wasn't the house for him.

For if it was, God would make it clear to him, right? Hopefully in a reasonable amount of time.

But God hasn't yet helped you with alleviating the guilt you carry around in not saving Tom, has He?

Quinton ignored the remorse that terrorized him day after day and focused on Isabelle. "Have you had many offers?"

"No, but this isn't the kind of house just anyone wants. I'm surprised more investors haven't eyeballed it. It could be a rental or something." She flashed him a flirty grin that he was sure she thought had some effect on him. But she was wrong. He'd never like Isabelle in that way. Especially not when she called him "Quinty." That just plain got on his nerves. "Are you thinking of purchasing it as an investment property?"

Quinton really didn't want to give Isabelle the details until he was sure of the path God was leading him down when it came to this house. "Not sure."

"Hmmm. You were always so evasive, Quinty."

He discounted her nickname for him and the fact that she thought she knew him so well. He sauntered through the rest of the house, mentally adding up the amount it would cost for each repair. And the time it would take to do the repairs. He would complete Irelynn's project soon, as well as, one of the houses in the Waterbury Acres Subdivision. That would open him up to work on this house until fall when he started the new house on Clark Avenue.

When he finished scrutinizing the inside, Quinton stepped out the front door and peered in the direction of Irelynn's house. He really would like her opinion on the place, if for nothing else, to give her some reassurance that he could and would make this house the best it could be for the twins. "Hey, Isabelle, there's someone down the street that I'm going to ask if she'd like to look at the house."

"Why?" Isabelle scrunched up her nose.

"I'd like to get her opinion on it too."

"Suit yourself. But don't take forever. I have another showing at 3:45."

Quinton took off at a jog toward Irelynn's house. Quicker even, than starting up the truck and driving there. Besides, he had some nervous energy he needed to expend.

Willing himself not to pull a muscle, he ran until he reached his destination and knocked on the door.

She appeared shocked to see him. "Quinton? The twins are still at Mom's this afternoon."

Irelynn thought he meant to retrieve the kids early. He shook his head and pointed his thumb down the street. "I'm looking at the house that's for sale before I pick up the kids, and I'd like your opinion on it."

Her face echoed suspicion. She truly did not trust him for whatever reason. Quinton pushed the somewhat discouraging thought aside. He wanted her trust him. "Look, Irelynn, I know you're concerned about the twins living there. It looks like a mess now, but if I buy it, I'll fix it up so it'll be like new. I would like your input, though, to see if you think it would work."

"All right." Irelynn slipped on her tennis shoes, grabbed her keys, and locked the door behind her.

"Wanna jog?" Quinton didn't want Isabelle to leave before they got there.

"Sure."

Together, in perfect sync, they jogged down the sidewalk, to the stop sign, then across the street to the house for sale. Quinton shrugged off the fact that he liked running with her. A lot. Even if it was just for a block.

Quinton held open the front door, and he and Irelynn stepped inside. Isabelle stood in the kitchen texting furiously on her phone. "I just love these back-and-forth negotiations," she quipped.

"Isabelle, this is my..." friend? No, not really. Hadn't Irelynn mentioned they weren't friends? Acquaintance? That sounded weird. He cleared his throat. "This is Irelynn Brady. I wanted to get her take on the house."

Isabelle gave Irelynn the once-over. "I see. I'm Isabelle Vacura, the top real estate sales agent in Chokecherry Heights for two years running." She slipped a hand Irelynn's way.

Irelynn graciously shook her hand.

Quinton watched and mentally compared the two women. Irelynn came out the obvious winner.

"Come along, I'll show you the place." She waved one hand at them and stuck her other arm through Quinton's elbow. "Quinty and I have known each other forever. Haven't we, Quinty?"

Quinton cringed once again at her nickname. He needed to tread carefully if to avoid jeopardizing the potential sale. "Since high school."

Isabelle's shrill laugh echoed in the near-empty home. "From precisely freshman year, but who's keeping track?" She announced each room to them, never taking her arm from his elbow, even in tight spaces. "Did you give any more thought to our theater date in the city?" she asked.

"I haven't."

Isabelle rolled her eyes and tossed a look Irelynn's way. "Quinty and I love the theater, but he works so hard at his job. It's difficult to tear him away from his work so we can have a date once in a while."

Irelynn's expression was priceless. What must she be thinking? Hopefully she didn't believe Isabelle. Quinton never had and never would like the theater. "Isabelle, you know that..."

"And he's such a dear to want to buy this place. He has always seen the potential in projects, whether houses or people." Isabelle pursed her lips. "So, what do you think, Irelynn?"

"I think it needs a lot of work, but it does have potential."

Kudos to Irelynn. He appreciated her positive outlook.

"I thought these two rooms would work for Mia and Max and this would be an incredible master bedroom. I'd knock out that wall and..."

"Absolutely outstanding. You already know what to do to

accommodate the people who will be living here." She tightened her grip on his arm. "Isn't he the ambitious one?" Without waiting for an answer from Irelynn, Isabelle continued. "There's an entire downstairs too. Just wait until you see it. It makes the upstairs look like a five-star hotel." Isabelle finally released her hand from Quinton's elbow as they made their way down the stairs to the basement.

"This would make an ideal living room and off to the corner, I'd build in a room for a home office." At Quinton's comment, Irelynn's face lit up.

"A home office would be awesome."

Another thing they agreed on? Nicole would appreciate that for sure.

"So, just what is it that you do, Irelynn?" Isabelle tilted her head toward Irelynn, her tone condescending.

"I build websites for companies."

"Oh. I see."

"I think that's impressive. No one would cut me loose with coding and graphic design," said Quinton.

"No, Quinty, probably not. But you do have a gift for building things with wood." Isabelle fluttered her eyes at him and Quinton wanted to puke. She really needed to stop with the flirting. Once this house was a done deal, he'd set Isabelle straight on a lot of things.

"What do you think, Irelynn?"

For some odd reason, he wanted Irelynn to like the place, not as it was in its current state, but rather what it could be. To give him some incentive to purchase it. Even if she didn't want him living down the street from her.

Her opinion mattered. The realization of that fact baffled him.

"It has potential, and I think your ideas are valid. I've seen what you can do with new construction and what you've done so far with the kids' rooms, so I say go for it."

Just what he needed to hear. Maybe Irelynn wasn't so bad after all. A ton better than Isabelle and all her fakeness.

"Even if it's just down the street from you?"

She hesitated. Maybe she'd changed her mind. Quinton held his breath.

"Wait a minute," interrupted Isabelle. "You are going to live in this dump?" Her tweezed eyebrows arched.

"Yes, Isabelle, I am."

Poor Isabelle looked like she might lose consciousness. "I do apologize, but I have another showing in 15 minutes. I really must be going." She led them from the house. "Do call me tonight. We should discuss this."

The only thing Quinton would be calling Isabelle about was to make an offer on the house.

"MOM, it's the craziest idea ever. He wants to buy the house for sale down the street."

Mom's eyes widened. "Oh, dear. The squalid one with the tall weeds that looks condemned?"

"That's the one."

"Sounds serious. I'll put on some coffee."

Minutes later, Irelynn took a sip of freshly-brewed coffee. "It is serious, Mom. I mean, that's too close for my taste."

"I was thinking more about that poor house. It might fall down."

"Mom, really. What about the fact that he will be right down the street? As in, *right down the street?*"

"I thought the two of you were getting along better."

Irelynn tossed a glance at Mia and Max who had dragged out the toybox and had toys scattered everywhere. Had Mom gone shopping again for toys for her grandchildren?

"We are getting along better, but I still don't like him." Not really. Or at least not that much.

"Oh. How disappointing. I sure do like Gram."

"Mom, you can like Gram whether Quinton and I are friends or not."

Mom appeared to ponder that. "True. Perhaps Quinton is thinking of the convenience of it all."

"He is. That and it's close to the pathways since he's a runner."

"Hmmm. Just like someone else I know. Could it be that you two have something in common?" Mom didn't wait for Irelynn's objection. "No wait, you have several things in common. You both love God, the twins, pizza, and running. Is that four things?"

"Mom, you're not helping. Whose side are you on anyway?"

"Your side, dear. Always your side. I'm loyal to a fault. You know that. I'm just being realistic here. Now, is the house safe for the children?"

Irelynn cringed. "Not as it is at the present moment. The place is gross. But I do know that Quinton can fix it up and make it look nice. He does have that talent. I've seen the new house he's building too, and it's phenomenal."

"Did you just say something positive about your nemesis?"

"Shh, Mom, don't let word get out."

Mom laughed. "If you think he can fix it up to where it's safe for the children, as that is our number one priority, is it not?"

"Yes."

"Then would it be so bad to have him that close? Think of the ease when they get older, especially."

"My mother. The voice of reason."

Mom beamed. "I earned that title."

"And get this. The real estate agent calls him 'Quinty' and insinuates they're an item." Although why that bothered her, she didn't know. Quinton could date that uppity Isabelle for all she cared.

Right?

"Really?" asked Mom.

"Yes. She practically hangs all over him. She's gorgeous and I felt like a country bumpkin next to her in my workout clothes."

"I didn't realize Quinton had a girlfriend. Gram never mentioned it."

Irelynn sucked in her breath. "Do you and Gram talk about us?"

"We've been known to mention you two a time or two."

"What do you talk about?"

"Not much." Mom shrugged, but it was a rather suspicious shrug in Irelynn's opinion.

"Mom, please tell me the two of you aren't getting any ideas."

"Ideas? No, although you two really could be a…"

"No, absolutely not. You know he's my nemesis and he's an irritant." *Although slightly less so in recent days.*

Mom snickered. "An irritant. Who knew my daughter was such a comedian." Her face grew serious. "I'm hearing what you're saying about the house and the close proximity to Quinton. It's definitely something to lift up in prayer. I have heard that sometimes when people live in the same town or live really close by that they actually see each other less than if they lived farther apart. Perhaps that's how it will be for the two of you. Especially if he and the real estate agent are dating, they may someday get married. Then you wouldn't have to worry so much about Quinton, as he'd be preoccupied with his 'other' family. Not that the twins would be a secondary priority, but his time wouldn't be as free as it is now."

Quinton marrying Isabelle? Quinton marrying anyone? Having another family?

An odd feeling swelled in her chest and Irelynn no longer desired the remainder of her coffee.

Must be because Nicole wouldn't have chosen someone like Isabelle Vacura to help raise Mia and Max.

CHAPTER 13

It was the fourth round of Uno with Gram and her friends, and so far, Quinton was tied with Miss Bea, the honorary Uno champion.

"Tell you what, Quinton," quipped Miss Bea, "Let's you and me make a bet on this last game."

"What about us?" Mrs. Pierce leaned forward and looked over the edge of her glasses that were brand new in 1940.

Miss Bea appeared thoughtful. "If Quinton wins, he chooses the game for next week. Why, I'll even give up Uno if that's what it takes." Miss Bea took a deep sigh, as if she'd made some huge sacrifice. "I'll play any game except one of those board games. Now, if one of us wins..." Miss Bea pointed to herself, then to Gram and Mrs. Pierce. "If one of us wins, Quinton has to ask that sweet girl out on a date."

Quinton couldn't believe Gram and her friends were once again discussing this topic. Was nothing sacred? "What sweet girl?"

"The one with the country-sounding name. What is it? England? Spain?" Miss Bea appeared perplexed. "No, not those. It's Ireland."

"Irelynn?" Quinton asked.

Gram smirked. "She's the one."

Quinton shot Gram a dirty look. "Have you been talking about me liking Irelynn?" The thought horrified him for more reasons than one.

"No." But Gram's face was rather sheepish. "She's just such a nice gal. So Godly and kind, and she loves those kids."

"Gram..."

"Yes, that's the one," agreed Miss Bea. "If one of us wins, you ask her out. It's high time you settled down, young man, what with those children in your care." She paused and stuck out her wrinkled hand with white-tipped manicured nails toward Quinton. "Deal?"

"Yes," chorused Gram and Mrs. Pierce.

"Wait. What about me?" Quinton ignored Miss Bea's hand, waiting for Gram to chastise him for his rudeness.

Miss Bea ignored him, pulled her hand back in, and dealt the cards.

What had he gotten himself into?

Quinton lost, to Gram no less, and did his best to get out of the bet he never agreed to make.

To no avail.

"You have to keep your end of the bargain," whispered Gram. "It's the gentlemanly thing to do."

Might be harder than he could even imagine. "I suppose Nicole would appreciate us getting along."

Gram's quirked eyebrows indicated she didn't believe his motivating factor.

Problem was, he wasn't so sure he wasn't so sure he believed it himself.

～

A HALF-HOUR LATER, Quinton and Gram drank root beer floats in Gram's apartment. No more mention of the date was made, as Gram had declared it a settled issue.

But for Quinton, it was anything but a settled issue.

He'd tried every argument he could think of with his mind barely functioning after a long day of work and two hours spent with Gram's crazy friends. How could he go on a date with someone he didn't even like? Wasn't The Pizza Slice "date" sufficient? What about the kids? Gram had an answer for that one. "Take them with you," she chortled.

Quinton did his best not to get irritated with his precious Gram, but really, this was pushing it too far. Besides, Irelynn would never agree.

He dreaded the thought of even asking her. He'd invited her to The Pizza Slice, but that had been different. This was assumed to be a date all because of Miss Bea and Mrs. Pierce.

The things he did for Gram.

"Let's talk about something else, dear. What did you ever decide on the house down the street from Irelynn's? Did you choose that one or the other one?"

"I've prayed a lot about this, and have spoken with the leader of our men's ministry at church." Quinton paused. "After crunching the numbers, I think I can afford to purchase the one by Irelynn's house and completely remodel it. But I'm going to negotiate the asking price."

"Good for you. It sure doesn't hurt to make an offer. They might accept it just to get out from under it."

"I agree. It's not like everyone is wanting that house. It's in poor shape, but nothing that can't be fixed."

Gram smiled. "Ah, now that's my grandson. Just like his father, never did see a house that was beyond repair. Kind of like how God sees us. No one is too far beyond His redemption."

"True. I hadn't thought of that."

"Yes, well, I'm thrilled for you. I'll pray they accept the lower offer. But do you think it'll be too much of an undertaking with all of your other projects?"

"It seems overwhelming right now, but if I chip away at it, I think it's attainable. My landlord will let me rent the apartment until I need to move out, so there's no rush there. I want the house to be safe for the kids."

Gram nodded. "And you'll be finished with Irelynn's remodel, so that will also free up some time."

"Yes." Why did the thought of being done with the twins' rooms at Irelynn's bum him out just a bit?

"What is it you young people say? Go for it?"

Quinton laughed. "Something like that."

"I have confidence in you, Quinton. You'll be able to make this house a home for the twins."

Gram's confidence in him was all he needed.

IRELYNN SUSPECTED something unusual about Quinton when he arrived on Thursday. Something about the suspicious glint in his blue eyes.

Made him all the more handsome. Not that she was noticing whether he was handsome or homely.

"Hey, Irelynn."

"Hi, Quinton."

He shifted from side to side. Was her nemesis nervous? That would be a first. He always seemed so confident. So self-assured.

"The twins are down for a nap, but they'll be up soon. I'm sure they'll be thrilled to see you."

"Yep."

"I guess I should finish the dishes while they're sleeping."

Quinton cleared his throat. "Look, Irelynn. Would you like to go get some ice cream with me?"

Ice cream? With him.

Um. No.

Although, it did sound like it might be enjoyable.

Sort of.

"I mean, not like a date or something. With the kids. Kind of like the The Pizza Slice thing we did."

"What a relief. I'm glad you clarified it's not a date. In that case, sure."

"Great."

Awkwardness lingered in the air. "Were you thinking today?"

"Yes. There's that popular ice cream stand over on Main Street."

Irelynn knew the one. She and Mom had stopped there once. "All right. Well, I better get these dishes done."

"I better work on the rooms. I'm installing new windows today. We're getting closer to the finish line with this remodel."

"That'll be nice to have it done so you won't have to stop here more often than necessary."

His face held an expression she couldn't quite decipher. "Yeah."

QUINTON STARTED up his truck and began the drive to the ice cream stand. He was rarely an anxious person, but asking Irelynn to join him for ice cream had set his otherwise manly nerves on edge. Perhaps it was because Miss Bea and Mrs. Pierce had considered it a date and would likely be asking for a report on how it went. But hadn't the time he took Irelynn to see the house he was building in Waterbury Acres, followed by the time at The Pizza Slice more like a date than a spontaneous trip to the ice cream stand?

She looked really pretty today with her hair down around her face. Not that he was noticing, but he had sort of observed it wasn't in a ponytail. Maybe that's why the whole thing was embarrassing. Then when they just stood there looking at each other without saying a word...

"Can I have the pink-and-blue ice cream?" Mia asked when they reached the ice cream stand window with its long list of flavors posted on the wall.

"Cotton candy?" Irelynn said.

"Yes, cott candy!"

"What kind do you want, Max?" she asked.

"Chocwit."

"You're just like Gram, Max. Chocolate is her favorite too. What about you, Irelynn?"

"Cookies and cream."

"That will be one cotton candy, one chocolate, and one cookies and cream. For you, sir?" the clerk asked him.

"I'll have cookies and cream too."

Irelynn shot him an incredulous look. "You like cookies and cream too?"

"It's my favorite."

She appeared doubtful.

"No, really. Guess it's another thing we have in common."

THEY BOTH DECLARED their favorite pizza to be pepperoni, both loved cookies and cream ice cream, were both runners, and loved table hockey. What a blessing those were the only things they had in common.

Irelynn directed Mia and Max to a picnic bench while she and Quinton carried their ice creams to avoid any mishaps along the way. The twins sat down and contentedly ate their desserts before heading toward the fenced-in mini playground area.

A couple sat down on the other side of the bench, causing Quinton to scoot closer to Irelynn so their arms touched. His proximity made her heart beat crazily in her chest.

Bizarre and troubling that he would have that effect on her.

Irelynn was right-handed, and he was left-handed. Not a favorable combination for eating ice cream. Thankfully, she had dumped her double scoop of cookies and cream into a bowl or it was likely the entire dessert would end up on her turquoise shirt.

She was eating and enjoying watching the children play when she noticed Quinton staring at her. Irelynn met his gaze. He did have nice eyes; she'd give him that. She watched as his stare went from her eyes to her mouth.

Was he thinking of kissing her?

Why was the thought even occurring to her?

To kiss her nemesis? It would be horrific to say the least.

Or would it?

Would she want him to kiss her?

Quinton's words interrupted her thoughts. "Uh, you..."

"Yes?"

He leaned closer.

Maybe she was starting to like him, just a little. But to let Quinton kiss her?

Irelynn held her breath.

"You have some ice cream."

"Ice cream?" she squeaked. Of course, she had ice cream. That's what they had come here for.

"You have ice cream dripping down your chin." In an instant motion, Quinton took his thumb and wiped away the drizzling ice cream.

"Oh." Irelynn let out a big sigh. He hadn't wanted to kiss her at all. Thankfully.

Why then did she experience the teensiest tiniest bit of disappointment?

"Here, you might need these." He handed her a stack of napkins.

Just great. What else might she have on her face and not know it? He probably thought she was someone with a drooling condition. She should change the subject. Quickly.

Quinton had faced forward to watch Mia and Max again. What should they talk about to remedy this cringeworthy moment? Finally, it came to her. "I forgot to tell you I took Max to the doctor. She said exactly what my mom had suspected. Max doesn't talk much because Mia does all the talking."

"Typical girl."

Irelynn tossed him a look, but couldn't be mad at him. Not when his eyes twinkled that way.

What? Twinkling eyes? Remember, Irelynn, this is your somewhat-of-a-nemesis. Granted, his nemesis factor has fallen to 85 percent, still...

"Irelynn?"

She snapped back from her argument with herself and glanced up at him. "I'm sorry, what?"

"I said, are the kids doing better at night? With the nightmares and stuff?"

"They are. They still have their moments with the nightmares, and they ask a lot of questions about Nicole, which is hard. But I think they're doing better. What about when you have them?"

Quinton nodded. "They're doing better. It'll take some time, though."

"That's what the doctor said. They've lost so much."

"At least we can give them a loving home."

The way he combined them together as a team left an odd feeling in her chest. But they were a team in a sense.

And something about that didn't bother her as much as it once had.

CHAPTER 14

Irelynn and the twins made it a point to visit Mrs. Caruthers and take her cookies once every couple of weeks. The eccentric older woman still didn't elaborate on what she kept inside her secret notebook. Nor did she complain about the frequency of their visits.

"Mrs. Brady, I'm so glad you came over today."

Irelynn had given up explaining to Mrs. Caruthers that she was "Miss Brady," not "Mrs. Brady," and Quinton's last name was "Gregory," not "Brady."

Mrs. Caruthers took a deep breath and set the plate of cookies on a plastic table near the door. "You see, as the Neighborhood Lookout Society president, I am assigned tasks that can, at times, be difficult and a considerable challenge, even for the best of us."

The woman belonged in a movie or a book as the lead character. "We're thankful for all you do for the neighborhood, Mrs. Caruthers."

"Naturally, we all have a calling put upon us in life, and this is mine. I was married to my beloved, but ornery, Herman for nearly 50 years, bless his soul. When he passed, I knew I must undertake the important mission I was never able to while he was alive." She held out both hands in a gesture encompassing the surrounding vicinity. "You see, I have to keep an eye on the comings and goings in the neighborhood and keep us all safe."

"For that we are grateful."

"Yes, and the other day, I was out watering my flowers in the front yard, when I saw someone looking at the old ramshackle home that has been up for sale for exactly a year and four months last Friday. By the way, a full disclosure just between you and me," she lowered her voice to barely above a whisper, "my eyesight is not what it used to be."

Irelynn nodded, wondering what Mrs. Caruthers was about to divulge.

"I stood on the porch chair, carefully, mind you, as I don't need a broken bone at my age, and attempted to see the distance between my house and the dilapidated house." Her voice returned to its normal octave. "I decided the best plan of action was to retrieve Herman's binoculars. So that is what I did. I peered through his prized binoculars he received as an award for selling the most tractors at the Chokecherry Heights Tractor Store back in '75." With a vibrant purple fingernail, she edged her thick-rimmed glasses further up the bridge of her nose. "Anyhow, I saw a young man walking around the perimeter of the home. Mind you, he seemed somewhat familiar, but I couldn't place him, not with my vision distorted. Have you ever looked through a pair of binoculars while wearing glasses?"

"No, Mrs. Caruthers, I actually have not."

"Didn't think so. It's downright impossible. Oh, how I wish I fully understood how to take pictures with my phone. My grand-daughter showed me the zoom-up-close function one time, but I can't for the life of me get my phone to cooperate. Not that it would have mattered anyway because I didn't have my phone with me at the moment. But I digress." Mrs. Caruthers took a deep breath.

Irelynn dared to focus her attention on Mia and Max. "That tickled my nose," giggled Mia, as she leaned over to sniff the flowers. Flowers that were slightly less upright than moments earlier. She shook her head at the twins, praying they would leave Mrs. Caruthers's flowers intact.

"Because I forgot to bring my phone outside," continued Mrs. Caruthers, "I decided to do a professional sketch of the individual I saw at the home. I'll be presenting my findings at the Neighborhood Lookout Society meeting next Thursday. I know you aren't yet a member, but I find it only fitting for you to see the sketch since this could be our newest neighbor in the neighborhood. Sure, this man will reside a block away, but one can never be too careful, especially with children." She nodded at Mia and Max who were poking around at the flowers.

Irelynn hoped they wouldn't pick any.

"Wait right here, Mrs. Brady, and I'll show you the sketch." She rushed into the house, only to return with a notebook, different from the one in which she took notes. "Now, I was nearly hired by law enforcement years ago as a forensic artist due to my extraordinary ability to create likenesses with my art."

"That's impressive, Mrs. Caruthers."

"Yes, but wait until you see the sketch." She flipped open the notebook to a page with a drawing of a person. "Here's the man."

Irelynn couldn't really tell who the man was from the sketch. It was just a step up from a stick-figure drawing.

"And here's his truck. Something about it does ring a distant bell, but these days all trucks look the same to me, especially from this distance." The elderly woman pursed her lips. "What with Ida Mattson's overgrown lilac bush partially obstructing my vision, my view of the truck was limited to just the far back portion of it."

Sure enough, Mrs. Caruthers had drawn only the rear portion of the truck.

"I've used some pencil shading to add depth and dimension to the truck sketch." She paused. "Do you recognize the man or his truck?"

"I can't say as I do, Mrs. Caruthers. Sorry."

"Be sure to keep an eye out for him. I'll be doing preliminary investigations. It's so much easier now that I have taken lessons on how to use the internet. Before, it was tedious hours of digging through records at the county courthouse."

Irelynn wondered if Quinton knew someone else was interested in the house. He'd been so excited about it. While it was probably best he didn't purchase it, she could admit there would be a few positives to having him nearby.

"HEY, IRELYNN," Quinton greeted, as he walked into the house the following day with his toolbox. "This is one of my employees, Troy. He'll be doing the painting in the rooms. Troy, this is Irelynn Brady."

Irelynn extended her hand, and Troy shook it. His piercing, almost hardened, dark eyes seemed to bore a hole right through her. "Nice to meet you."

"You too." He tugged at his scruffy red beard. "Time to get to work."

"Have a good time on your run," Quinton said.

"Thanks."

"Maybe next time I can join you and the twins."

Irelynn shrugged. "All right." Maybe it wouldn't be so bad to run with Quinton. She dismissed the notion that maybe her feelings for him were changing for the better.

She called to the twins and left Quinton and Troy to work in the house.

Irelynn pulled the baby jogger from her meager one-car garage, all the while keeping an eye on Mia and Max who played in the front yard with a soccer ball. She unfolded the stroller and paused for a moment, taking in the sight of the twins. Mia twirled around in circles and sang a song from their children's church class. Max kicked the ball toward his sister, glee on his flushed cheeks. "Mia, kick ball," he said.

"No, I'm a bol-rina."

"Mia, kick ball, pease?"

Mia interrupted her twirling just long enough to kick the ball back to Max.

Irelynn swallowed hard. The children's futures depended on her and Quinton. The course of their young lives hinged on the choices made by surrogate parents chosen by a mother who had known her children for but a breath in a lifetime cut short by a terminal illness.

The realization threatened fear and doubt to settle once again within the confines of Irelynn's heart and mind.

Such a mind-boggling responsibility for two people who had no clue the extent such an obligation would entail.

A tear slid down her face. She felt so unworthy of this awesome responsibility. So unsure at times, so uncertain how to manage being a mom. Yet, gratitude permeated her thoughts.

She had always longed to be a mom. To love her children the way her own mom loved her. The unconditional love, the sacrifices, and the shaping of a future generation. To raise them for the Lord.

God held the future of the twins in His hands. Had created them as tiny womb-mates over three years ago. He knew the path their lives would take. He knew the outcome of the tragedy that had overtaken them before they had a chance to fully know their parents.

He is faithful. Always faithful. Her mom's words seeped into her mind, as they often did in times of uncertainty. God was faithful. He would make a way.

Max somersaulted in the grass, one after the other. After

several, he attempted to stand, veering from side to side from the dizzying effects of his gymnastics.

Mia giggled and did her own somersaults.

Irelynn remained in the porch's shadow, witnessing the playful antics of the twins. Someday, she hoped to get married and have children of her own. Quinton would likely do the same. Was the real estate agent his girlfriend? Would they someday get married? Irelynn pondered how their future marriages would impact the custody arrangement.

And why did the thought of him having a girlfriend leave her with an empty feeling? It wasn't like she cared one way or the other what Quinton did in his personal life as long as he was an exemplary father to the children.

Right?

At least they were getting along better. Nicole would appreciate their efforts, even if they would never be more than friends. Despite Nicole's prodding and Mom's suggestion that Quinton was a "good catch," as she called him in her archaic terms.

A good catch for someone, but definitely not for her.

Max tugged on her shirt. "Are we going to pwayground?"

"Yes, we are. Please get in the stroller and I'll grab your snacks." She buckled them into the stroller and handed them their special snacks specifically for times when they rode in the stroller. They typically devoured the healthy treats before they left the driveway. From the excitement on their faces, this time would be no different.

It was a win-win situation. A healthy stress-relieving run for her and playtime at the playground for them.

Irelynn verified she had the house keys and a water bottle. Wait. She'd forgotten the water bottle. Irelynn ran back inside to retrieve it from the kitchen. As she neared the cupboard, she heard Quinton and Troy talking, their voices echoing because of the empty room.

"It sounds like it's a royal pain to have to share the kids all the time," Troy said.

They have no idea I'm here.

"It is," agreed Quinton.

"My cousin is a custody lawyer. I could put you in touch with him and you could easily get full custody. Irelynn's not even related to the twins."

Should she wait for an answer from Quinton? Would he agree? What his friend said had merit. But how did Troy know she wasn't related to the twins? Had Quinton shared some of the details about the custody arrangement?

Hurt mixed with frustration filled her heart.

Irelynn grabbed the water bottle and retreated. She didn't want to take the chance on them catching her eavesdropping or hearing Quinton's answer. Would he agree with Troy?

Tears burned her eyes as she placed the water bottle in the holder on the stroller and pushed off, heading into a vigorous jog right away, against her better judgment. She couldn't even think about warming up and easing into the run. Not with what she had just heard.

True. She wasn't related to Mia and Max.

True. It was a hassle to shift them back and forth all the time.

True. It would be easy for Quinton to get full custody.

But Irelynn loved the twins and wanted to help raise them. And she had made a promise to Nicole, a promise she wouldn't break.

She thought things between her and Quinton were getting better. Hadn't they come to an understanding? Become somewhat friends, at least? Hadn't his nemesis factor dropped to an 85 percent?

But if Quinton had the mind to do so, it wouldn't be difficult for him to pursue this, and he hadn't said anything in response to what Troy said. Did he agree? Was he contemplating his employee's words?

The run down the pathways and toward the park was a blur. The tears ran faster now down her face, and Irelynn took extra care not to trip over something in her path. How could Troy be so calloused? She was doing the best she could.

Please, Lord, let that be enough.

CHAPTER 15

Quinton wasn't sure what happened between the time he'd arrived at Irelynn's house and the time she returned from her run. They'd gotten along so well since that night at The Pizza Slice, a night he'd remember as a turning point for them. They'd even gotten along when he'd asked her for her opinion of the house he wanted to purchase. Score two points for their amicable treatment of each other in recent days. And then the ice cream "date," which had gone smoothly too.

Whatever it was, Irelynn wasn't happy with him. He'd noticed that immediately. Troy had left after he and Quinton had finished putting the first coat of paint on the walls in Mia's room, but would return tomorrow. Quinton figured, while the guy wasn't his favorite, Troy did do a satisfactory job.

"Would you like to come see how the walls are coming along?" he asked Irelynn after she and the twins returned.

She followed him but said nothing. Only nodded. Did she not think he and Troy did an adequate job? While painting wasn't his strong suit, he did have Troy's assistance during the first part of the afternoon, and painting *was* Troy's strong suit, or else Quinton wouldn't have hired him for the myriad of painting projects in the various houses Quinton built and remodeled.

"What do you think?" he asked, hoping to elicit some response, even if it wasn't the response he hoped for.

Irelynn stood not far from him in the humble room. Quinton looked more closely at her. Her shoulders slumped and her face was puffy, like she'd been crying. "It looks fine," was all she said before she turned away from him.

"Irelynn, are you all right?"

Hurt filled her eyes. Had someone been mean to her? Had she injured herself on the run? She didn't appear injured. Had the twins had another of their tantrums? "I'm fine." Her voice came across as almost a snap.

Excuse him for caring.

Irelynn avoided eye contact. "I need to check on Mia and Max."

Quinton watched her go. Should he go after her and ask her again? Offer to help her with whatever bothered her? That day they'd gone out for pizza, she'd been all upset. Maybe this was the same issue. Perhaps unresolved?

He sure couldn't understand women. Another reason why he had no desire to ever marry. Too much hassle trying to comprehend their complex ways.

QUINTON SAT across from Isabelle at Your New Residence Real Estate Agency. She touched his forearm with her hand. "I'm so glad you're here, Quinty. It's fabulous to spend more time with you."

He wanted to tell her the only reason he was here was to hopefully sign the paperwork and put the house under contract. But he'd wait a smidgen longer before doing anything to jeopardize the sale.

Not that there weren't other houses on the market if this one fell through, but its location was just so *convenient.*

Even if the work to give the home a complete overhaul would be time intensive. Quinton hoped when he finished, it would be the house Mia and Max grew up in and even came back to visit with their own children.

Yep, it was the "planner" in him. He wanted a home for them to come back to—for them to remember the fond memories Quinton hoped to cultivate.

"Quinty?"

Quinton looked up to meet Isabelle's gaze. "Yes?"

"Wasn't sure where you went for a moment." She flipped her hair behind her shoulder, an obvious habit of hers, and gave him a flirtatious wink. When he didn't respond, Isabelle continued. "Chokecherry Heights National Bank was extremely hesitant to accept your ridiculously low offer. You see, they feel the home is worth much more than what you offered. However, I did remind them of all the work to be done if the house even passes inspection. They then readily agreed to your low offer. I, too, am taking a substantial hit in my commission, but it's worth it for you."

Awww, thanks for the charity, Isabelle. "Thanks. I appreciate it."

"Anything for you, Quinty. So, both parties will sign the offer, and then we'll proceed with inspections and the bank loan paperwork." She paused and pooched her lips. "Do tell me again why you insist upon living in such a dive."

"Lord willing, it won't be 'such a dive' when I get finished remodeling it. I want the kids to have some stability in their lives, and I think this house is the perfect thing for that. Plus, it's in a convenient location with the paths and the park," *and a block away from Irelynn. Who is really angry at me right now, for no apparent reason.*

Isabelle held up a finger. "Whoa, hold on. What kids?"

"Mia and Max. Nicole's twins."

"Do you mean to tell me..."

"Yes, Isabelle, after Nicole passed, I was given joint custody of them."

Isabelle looked like she had just eaten something sour. "You are raising Nicole's twins?"

"Yes, with Irelynn."

"Irelynn, the dowdy woman you brought to look at the house with you?"

Irelynn may not deem Quinton on her "friend list" at the moment, but the insult Isabelle had just hurled at her didn't sit well with Quinton. He found himself wanting to defend her. "She's not dowdy, Isabelle, and yes, that's the woman."

"Hmmm. I think she's dowdy, but my opinion aside, why would Nicole have you both raising them? Unless...don't tell me you're dating her?" Isabelle leaned forward, her eyes bulging and her mouth falling open. The scent of her perfume overwhelmed the air and he stifled a sneeze.

"It was Nicole's wish, and you know I'd do anything for my sister. And no, I'm not dating Irelynn."

"We can thank our lucky stars above for that."

"Isabelle, do you mind if we proceed with the signing of the paperwork? I have another appointment at 10:45."

"Oh, sure. Yes." She slid the paperwork toward him and explained the contents. "Just a reminder, as I've mentioned to you before, I'm the seller's agent, so you are welcome to get your own buyer's agent if you wish."

"I'm good." Quinton scanned over the paperwork, praying for the Lord's wisdom and guidance. He'd spent plenty of prayers on this decision. It was no longer just himself he had to look out for. Now Quinton had two young children whose futures depended on his choices.

He shoved the stressful thoughts aside. He did not want to mess anything up. Quinton had to succeed at this at all costs. Nicole's trust in him that he could do this trumped all else.

Sticky yellow flag reminders flanked the signature lines.

Quinton signed each one, his signature a reminder he was about to become a homeowner. "Thanks for all your help on this, Isabelle."

"Sure. Oh, and since you're not dating that Irelynn woman, would you care to go out sometime?" Isabelle leaned toward him again, her face inches from his. "Your cologne is the same as you wore in high school. I love that scent."

He wasn't wearing any cologne, but Quinton didn't tell her that. It was obvious Isabelle would not give up on her quest, but he wanted none of it. "Thanks again. I should be going." Would she notice his, what he hoped was gentle, rebuff of her flirtation?

"All right." She scooted her chair back and stood, once again placing a hand on his forearm. "Do give me a call in the next day or so. We really should get together."

Quinton met Isabelle's gaze. How different she was from Irelynn, who was so classy and unassuming. And much prettier than Isabelle's high-maintenance appearance.

Whoa. Why are you thinking about Irelynn right now? Especially since she's not exactly happy with you for whatever reason.

Minutes later, Quinton climbed into his truck and headed to his meeting with a prospective client. His mind remained on Irelynn. For some reason, he really didn't want to be the one who'd caused her sorrow the other day.

Why it mattered to him, he hadn't a clue.

Probably because Nicole would want it to matter.

Yep, that was it.

CHAPTER 16

Irelynn scanned the part-time work-from-home job listings on her computer. Mom had the kids this afternoon so she could finish her one remaining website. She needed to secure other job.

Especially if Quinton thought she couldn't raise the children.

She may not be their biological relation; however, biology meant nothing to Irelynn. She loved Mia and Max as if she herself had given birth to them. She couldn't imagine life without them.

But how to convince Quinton she should remain sharing joint custody of them? Did he believe, as Troy apparently did, that Irelynn should have no place in raising them? He hadn't responded to Troy's comment, after all. However, Quinton must have shared his frustrations with Troy, or the man wouldn't have brought up the subject in the first place.

The entire episode had played over and over in Irelynn's mind.

So much for trying *not* to be an overthinker. She certainly needed God's help with that.

Still, if Quinton hired a lawyer, she'd have to do the same. Where would she get the funds for that expenditure? She could barely pay her current bills.

Her fingers flicked across the keyboard as she did her best to focus on the task at hand, rather than the conversation she'd overheard.

FORTUNATELY, Quinton hadn't stopped by to work on the rooms for the past two days. It was just as well. Irelynn didn't want to talk with him. Didn't want to rehash what she'd heard and whether or not it was true. Because if it was, it would be too painful.

So, right or wrong, she avoided the situation.

Add that to the mixture of feelings zipping through her from the time spent at the ice cream stand. Had she really been in her right mind wanting him to possibly kiss her?

Irelynn shook her head. She'd only been able to briefly chat with Mom about what she'd overheard when Irelynn delivered Mia and Max to Mom's house earlier. Mom had offered reassurance, but the entire thing still bothered Irelynn.

She tapped away on her keyboard. Another half hour and Mom and the twins would arrive. She completed the coding, then paused to take a look at what she just added.

A song by her favorite Christian music artist blared through her ring tone, and she glanced at the number. It was a local one, but wasn't one she recognized, so Irelynn let it go to voicemail. There was no way she'd get all she needed to accomplish done if she took the time to answer the phone, especially since this was the third time in the past hour three different people had called.

A blip sounded, alerting her the caller had, indeed, left a voicemail message. Irelynn glanced at her watch. Twenty minutes.

With six minutes to spare, Irelynn finished the website. *Not too bad, if I do say so myself.* She hoped the customer would like it.

She stared at the rooms, noting the progress. Soon, Quinton

would be 100 percent finished with the remodel. No more visits from him except for when he retrieved or returned the children.

So why then was there a sliver of disappointment?

There shouldn't be, especially in light of the eavesdropped conversation between him and Troy.

Irelynn pushed the thought aside and took a deep breath. Five minutes until Mom arrived, and she was never late. She logged into her cell phone. This might be the only time she'd have a chance to check her messages until she put Mia and Max to bed. Evenings tended to be crazy busy.

Irelynn punched in her voicemail password and put her cell phone on speaker. "You have three unheard messages," the recording indicated. "First message, sent today at 3:10 p.m...." Irelynn deleted the telemarketer's call and listened to the second message. This one was from the women's ministry leader from church reminding Irelynn about an upcoming event. An unknown caller left the third and final message. "Hello, Miss Brady, this is Karla Eisle from Eisle Law Firm. Would you please give me a call at your earliest convenience?" Ms. Eisle provided her number.

Why was an attorney calling her?

Irelynn feared her heart had stopped. Was Quinton seeking sole custody after all? Would he go against Nicole's one-year wish?

And just when I was hoping I had just incorrectly overheard the conversation between him and Troy.

The plastic clock on the wall indicated it was one minute past 5:00 p.m. Too late to call a law firm. She'd have to worry about it all night and call in the morning.

A tap on the door indicated Mom and the twins had arrived. All it would take was for Mom to ask how the day went and Irelynn would lose it. The tears were that close to the surface.

"Hi, Aunt Irelynn," beamed Mia. "Look what we made."

"Look what we made," Max echoed, pointing at the crafty pictures created with macaroni noodles.

"Those are beautiful. We'll hang them on the fridge." To Mom, she added, "I remember making that same craft years ago."

"Who knew I'd be teaching my grandchildren about the delights of colored macaroni noodles?" Mom smiled, as the twins dashed toward their toys. "When they get older, I can't wait to teach them how to make a variety of pasta dishes."

Irelynn did her best to laugh at Mom's multiple-use strategy for colored noodles, but it didn't work.

She lost her composure.

"What's the matter, honey?" Mom's arm went around her shoulders.

"I had a call today from an attorney here in town. Karla Eisle. I let it go to voicemail because I was finishing up a website, and now it's too late to return the call. Oh, Mom. What if Quinton is going after sole custody after all?"

Mom placed a hand on Irelynn's arm. "Sounds serious. I'll go put coffee on and get the kids settled with some books."

Irelynn nodded and plopped down on her used couch in the living room. What would she do if she didn't have Mom? The one who had raised her single-handedly with no support from her father? The one who had always been there for her regardless of whatever problem Irelynn faced?

Irelynn heard Mom say something in a hushed tone to the twins, then open the cupboard and retrieve two coffee mugs.

Moments later, Mom reappeared with two steaming cups of coffee and handed one to Irelynn. "I put extra sugar in," she said with a wink.

Irelynn felt the tug of a teeny smile. "Thanks."

"Mia and Max are pilfering through the stack of books."

Irelynn eyed the children on the other side of the room. What would she do if she could no longer help raise them? If Quinton took them out of her life forever? "What am I going to do, Mom?"

"Well, for one thing," started Mom, "you're not going to worry about it."

"But, Mom, it's a big deal."

"It is a big deal, if that's what it is."

Irelynn squeezed her eyes tight, but the warm tears continued. "What else could it be?"

Mom took a sip. "Irelynn, let's not worry about this until you return the attorney's call. It could have nothing to do with custody at all."

"But after that conversation I overheard..."

"Right. That was concerning, but we don't know if Quinton agreed with his employee. Has he ever mentioned anything about it to you?"

Irelynn shook her head.

"You need to talk it over with Quinton."

"We don't exactly have conversations that often, especially not *deep* conversations, like this one would be."

"Perhaps it's time to talk to him about this. We can jump to conclusions all we want, but unless we speak with someone, we'll never know the truth for sure. I'm so sorry you overheard that, and you have every right to be hurt by Troy's words, but it's not necessarily true that Quinton agrees."

Mom did have a point. But how could Irelynn discuss something of this magnitude with him?

And to think they were getting along so much better before all this. "The good news is God already knows what's going to happen."

"I wish He'd let me in on the details." Irelynn took a sip of the coffee. True to her word, Mom had added more sugar, making the delicious brew sweeter.

"He doesn't tell us all that's going to happen because He wants us to trust Him."

"I know."

"Sometimes we know that, but it's hard to apply that knowledge. Let's pray about it, and tomorrow morning, call Ms. Eisle. If it is the scenario we're dreading, we'll tackle it."

Irelynn tossed her mom a skeptical look. "How would we do that?"

"It's not for us to worry about today. If and when a custody battle transpires, God will lead us in the right direction. I know that's hard. If I was you, I'd be scared too. But Nicole wanted you and Quinton to have joint custody. That counts for something."

"But I'm not related to them. And I'm struggling financially. It makes a perfect case for Quinton to raise them alone. And if he likes that real estate lady and marries her..."

"It's a lot to stress over, Irelynn, and I understand. When you were eight, your father called me one day threatening if I went after him for child support, he would seek sole custody of you."

"Really?" Irelynn hadn't known. She cringed. What if the courts had decided her father was the better parent for her? Irelynn's earliest memories of her dad were dismal at best.

"Yes. I was so filled with worry and scared to death. I couldn't rationalize that an honorable judge would ever see fit to allow an alcoholic who'd deserted you to raise you. All I could see was the storm that could brew if what your dad said was true."

"What happened?"

"I did my best to turn it over to the Lord, but believe me, it was tough. And sometimes it is. Trust is never easy." Mom paused. "After a week of being stressed out and unable to focus on anything else, I finally spoke to a lawyer. The fee for that one visit alone could have put groceries in our cupboard for almost two weeks. He assured me your dad would have an uphill battle if he decided to proceed with his plan. The lawyer asked if I wanted him to send a letter on my behalf, and I hired him to do so. I never heard from your dad again, and he changed his address just in case I let the child support office know about his whereabouts for all the present and back child support he owed me. None of which he ever paid."

"You never told me that story before, Mom."

"I tried not to say much about your dad. I wanted you to make a decision when you got older about how you felt about him without my influence." Mom sighed. "I'd like to say I was new in the faith when I was having those difficult times of trusting the Lord to handle the matter, but I'd been a Christian for a while by that time. He knows our struggles, Irelynn, and He cares about them all—the largest and the smallest concerns. But He also wants us to trust He will take care of us."

"I know, Mom, but sometimes it's tough. I love the kids so much."

"Yes, you do, and you're an amazing mom to them."

"I feel bad about ever complaining about their tantrums or bickering, or refusing to sleep at night."

Mom laughed. "If you didn't have a complaint once in a while about your kids' behavior, you wouldn't be human. Besides, aren't you and Quinton getting along better?"

Irelynn ignored the suspicious spark in Mom's eye. Her mother liked Quinton, and Irelynn could almost see the matchmaking possibilities churning through Mom's mind. "We were until I overheard the conversation."

"Any progress is an answer to prayer. And you've had a couple more website building jobs lately, correct? Even on top of what Jamie has given you?"

"Yes."

"Wonderful! And we discovered why Max wasn't speaking as much, and it's nothing serious. Definitely a praise."

"Mom, what are you getting at?" Irelynn would chuckle at Mom's guilty face if she wasn't so concerned about the whole custody thing.

Mom shifted on the couch. "What I'm getting at is that God has taken care of so many of your recent worries. Don't you think He can handle this one too?"

"Yes." But even in her own ears, her voice sounded unsure.

"I know it's hard, Irelynn."

"Quinton, at least, is a good dad."

"An excellent dad. But that doesn't mean you shouldn't continue to share in the raising of the children. At some point, you two will have to make choices about what's best for the twins, but with him moving only a block away, things will be so much easier."

Irelynn sighed. "I've actually thought about some things like that. For instance, when he marries or if I marry, and if we have other children."

"Yes, things like that. Things that will also be lifted to the Lord in prayer."

"Mom, thank you for caring about me and for having a strong faith."

Mom reached up and gently wiped a new tear. "Irelynn, I haven't always relied on the Lord. Relying on myself is much easier. But He has taught me much over the years, and He has been so patient and gracious with me."

"I'll try not to worry about it...until tomorrow."

"Irelynn..."

"Just joking, Mom."

Mom laughed. "All right then. After you call the attorney, please let me know. Remember, you're not in this alone."

What would she do without her mom? And more importantly, without her faith?

Quinton parked his truck in Irelynn's driveway. He sat for a moment to catch his breath. He knew he had some serious workaholic tendencies, and the lineup of jobs he had undertaken, including a new construction project, would only contribute to those tendencies.

A workaholic because he excelled at what he did? Or because it was an easy way to escape the guilt of not saving Tom? Whatever the reason, the concern needed to be addressed. He didn't want it to affect the twins. Thankfully, at this point with Irelynn assisting in their care, if he put in 15-hour days on the days he didn't have them, it didn't really matter.

But someday it would.

Quinton had been making strides in his therapy group regarding his PTSD, and he wanted to continue doing so. There was a lot going on in his life right now. Good in that it took his mind off of the guilt, but bad in that it threatened priorities.

Lord, please help me keep my priorities straight.

He'd need to hire a few more workers if business kept up at this pace.

Not that I'm complaining, Lord. The work enables me to provide for the twins, but I don't want it to become an idol.

And he wanted to undertake the remodel as well?

Lord, if that isn't what You have planned for me, let me know.

Fortunately, if all went as planned, renovating his house could take as long as he needed it to, so there was no rush. Also, there were many things he couldn't do—the plumbing and electrical upgrades and fixing the crack in the driveway, for instance.

Speaking of cracked driveways and dilapidated belongings, Quinton glanced over at Irelynn's mailbox. The battered-looking mailbox and the post on which it sat had sure seen better days. That's why he decided he would replace it today.

Not that Irelynn would probably care. She was angry at him for some reason he still couldn't quite figure out. Had he done something? Said something? Or was it that she was angry at something else and not him at all?

He fought caring because he did care. Something had happened at the ice cream date. Something in him had changed. As they sat together eating ice cream and watching Mia and Max play on the mini playground, Quinton realized one thing.

His feelings for Irelynn had changed.

Quinton was beginning to like her.

A lot.

As such, he wanted to help her out. Wanted her not to be mad at him.

He would tackle the mailbox in a few minutes. For now, he'd greet Irelynn and give the twins a big hug.

"Hi, Irelynn," he said when she opened the door. "Are the twins here?"

"No, they're with Mom. I'm finishing up a website."

"Oh."

She avoided eye contact, as she stepped out onto her front porch.

There was silence, and Quinton shifted to his other foot. "Well, uh..."

"Quinton?"

"Yes?"

"I love the twins." Her voice was quiet, almost like she was tearful.

"I know you do. I see it when you're with them." Why was she saying this?

"I just wanted you to know that even though I'm not related to them, I consider it a blessing and a privilege to care for them. I know it's rather unorthodox that we share them, but..."

"It's what Nicole wanted."

They stood on the porch, him confused about why she was trying to convince him she loved Mia and Max and looking like she might cry. "Irelynn, are you all right?"

She ushered him inside and closed the door. Probably in case Mrs. Caruthers was sneaking around taking notes again. "Quinton, I know you could demand full custody of them at any time. But I want you to know I will fight for them. I will fight to help raise them."

"What?"

"Yes, I will, and that's a promise. I love them too much to not be a part of their lives." She had planted her hands on her hips, trying to be strong, he supposed. Only it wasn't working. Tears slid down her face.

And Quinton had a strong urge to step forward and take her into his arms and remedy whatever bothered her. Instead, he planted his feet on the floor and his hands in his pockets. "I know you love them. I know you'd fight for them. That's why Nicole chose you." He paused. "What's this all about anyway?" His statement had come out harsher than he'd meant for it to.

Irelynn took a deep breath. Contemplating telling him, perhaps? "What is it, Irelynn?" Why couldn't women just come out and say what was wrong?

"I overheard you and Troy talking. He was saying something about how you should seek sole custody and that he had a cousin who was an attorney."

"Didn't you ever learn eavesdropping never amounts to anything good?" *Tamp down the harshness, Quinton*, he reprimanded himself. Even if the thought of her thinking so poorly of him that he'd take the kids away from her bothered him like nothing else, he needn't be brusque about it.

"Even if I have to eavesdrop, I'd rather find something out than be in the dark about it and find out before I could take proper action."

"There's nothing to find out about, Irelynn. I have no plans to seek full custody."

"But I overheard..." She paused. "You don't?"

"No. That never crossed my mind."

"But you didn't respond when Troy said that."

Quinton shook his head. "I didn't respond or you didn't overhear my response?"

She gave him a sheepish look.

"Exactly, Irelynn. You didn't overhear my response. I told Troy I wasn't interested in full custody. That Nicole wanted us to share Mia and Max and that her wishes were at the forefront. The only thing more important was the wellbeing of the twins."

Her expression told him she wasn't convinced. All he'd done was come over to fix her mailbox and finish the paint job in the rooms. Not to have a fight. But Quinton tackled things head on—always had—and he'd tackle this too. Until it was resolved.

"Then why did the attorney, Karla Eisle, call me?"

"I'm glad she called. Did you talk with her yet?"

"No, she left a message, and when I attempted to call her back, she was out of the office."

Quinton took a step toward her. She looked so vulnerable to him, with her shoulders burdened by this huge misunderstanding. Maybe he should he take her in his arms and fix it all.

Goodness knows he wanted to.

"Look, Irelynn. Karla is a friend of mine, but she was calling to have you build her a website. I told her about you and the incredible work you do. She never thought she needed a website before now because she mostly does local business, but I convinced her otherwise."

"Really?"

"Yes, really. Besides, she doesn't handle family law. She's into wills and trusts and that sort of thing."

"Oh." Her lip quivered, and that was his undoing. Quinton stepped forward and took her into his arms.

She sniffled. Was she crying? He leaned back and looked into her eyes. "You have nothing to worry about, Irelynn," he whispered.

"Thank you. I was just so scared. I don't want to lose the kids. I love them like they were my own."

Her words did something to him he couldn't explain. That this woman, his former rival, would love and care that much for children not biologically her own, but biologically related to him, endeared her to him all the more.

He wanted to kiss her.

But it for sure wasn't the appropriate time.

Far from it.

So instead, Quinton held her close and relished how she felt in his arms. Like a perfect fit. He planted a kiss on her forehead.

And realized something really profound.

He wasn't only developing feelings for Irelynn Brady.

He was falling in love with her.

CHAPTER 18

When the doorbell rang, Irelynn had jumped. Quinton's truck was parked on the driveway. She had forgotten he was coming over today to finish the painting job he and Troy started in Mia's room the other day.

Lord, help me know the right time to bring up the topic about the custody of the kids.

She detested confrontation, but the words had tumbled from her mouth before she could stop them. And now she rested peacefully in his arms, burdens lifted.

Trust didn't come easy to her, and Irelynn had spent some time last year speaking to the pastor about it. He mentioned it was likely due to the fact her dad left when she was young. Hopefully, she wasn't making a mistake in believing Quinton was a man of his word.

Thank You, Lord. Thank You that he isn't seeking sole custody. Please don't let me be wrong in trusting him.

She rested her head against his shoulder, held firmly in his embrace.

Had anything ever felt so right? Like she belonged there.

Wait. When did this happen? That I should be falling for my nemesis?

Quinton's words of consolation about not wanting to remove her from Mia's and Max's lives had dropped his nemesis factor from the 85 percent to around 10 percent, if at all.

Mixed emotions flooded her entire being. Gratitude, relief, and fondness.

He tenderly kissed her on the forehead and wiped one of the remaining tears with his thumb. "Never worry about that kind of stuff, Irelynn, and if you do, talk to me."

She could only nod for his gentle touch had rendered her speechless.

After what seemed like several minutes, Quinton took a step back from her and put his hands back in his pockets.

Already she missed the warmth and comfort of his embrace.

"So, your mailbox has seen better days. I noticed the other day the post looks like it might fall over in the next Chokecherry Heights windstorm."

He was still smiling at her. Over a mailbox. Her eyes connected with his. When Quinton smiled like that, he was irresistibly charming, she'd give him that. And a little too good-looking.

Okay, a lot good-looking.

"Yes, the mailbox post is rather rickety." She eyed it through the window, grateful for the change in subject. "The mailbox, too, has seen better days."

"No worries because I picked up a new post and a new mailbox today at Nathanson's."

He really is a thoughtful guy. How could I not have seen that before? "You didn't need to do that."

"Not a problem at all. Dad always said when you see a need, take care of it to the best of your ability. Putting in a new post and replacing the mailbox won't take much."

"I appreciate that. To be honest, I figured the mailman would someday lean too far out his window and take the entire contraption with him after dropping off the mail."

Quinton chuckled. Irelynn blushed.

And for a moment she forgot about their huge misunderstanding.

She counted the seconds, waiting for the moment to pass. Only the ticking of the clock filled the quiet room, as they stood facing each other.

Finally, he spoke again. "Is that cookies I smell?"

"Oops, I'd better check on those. I'd forgotten all about them baking in the oven when we were having our discussion."

"Discussion. That's one way to put it." He grinned at her again, and she nearly tripped over nothing, as she rushed to check the progress of the cookies.

"I mixed up a batch of chocolate crinkles this morning with the kids. I thought about taking over a plate to Mrs. Caruthers. I figure if I butter her up enough, she'll let me see all her secrets inside that notebook of hers."

Quinton chuckled again. He had a nice laugh.

"It would be interesting to see what she writes in there." He cleared his throat. "So, how about a few cookies in exchange for me replacing the mailbox?"

"And here I thought you would do it for free."

His blue eyes connected with hers again. And her heart did a flip-flop.

"I would do it for you even without cookies, but it might make me do the job more efficiently." His eyes twinkled.

"In that case, I'll get you a plate after they've had a chance to cool."

"It's a deal."

Still, neither of them moved.

A thought occurred to her—should she ask him how much the mailbox and post set her back? She'd been eyeballing all the charges at Nathanson's. At this point, Irelynn would be just shy of 117 years old when she paid off the bill.

She decided to wait.

And be grateful for a man who would fix it for her without even being asked.

Quinton pointed a thumb toward the direction of the mailbox. "Okay. I'll be right back." He sauntered out the door.

And she made a hasty escape to the kitchen.

~

QUINTON WHISTLED as he unloaded the post and the mailbox and put them on the lawn beside the old ones. A lot had happened in the course of a few minutes.

He'd reassured Irelynn he wasn't seeking full custody. Like that would ever even cross his mind. *Thanks, Lord, for straightening out that mess.*

And he'd realized she wasn't so bad after all.

Maybe not bad at all.

Quinton likened it to when he first started a new home or remodel job. He didn't know how the entire project was going to turn out; just knew it would. With Irelynn he hadn't known how they would ever become friends, just known they probably would at some point.

But somewhere along the way, they'd skipped the friendship portion. Because what he thought of her went beyond friendship.

And her smile. Wow. When she smiled, it lit up her entire face.

All this time, Quinton had thought of Irelynn as his rival, but then today after holding her in his arms and being so close to her...

Could Nicole have been right about them having a chance together?

Don't get ahead of yourself there, Quinton, my man, he chastised himself.

The sound of a screen door shutting interrupted his thoughts.

He glanced up to see Mrs. Caruthers standing on her front porch with her notebook. Quinton waved. "Hello."

Mrs. Caruthers adjusted her glasses and merely nodded at him.

If he was going to move into this neighborhood, Quinton would have to befriend all the neighbors.

Even odd ones that appeared suspicious and recorded every breath taken in the neighborhood.

Quinton would finish his task with record speed. It wasn't so much the cookies that enticed his efficient work, or the fact he had a couple hours of painting ahead of him. No, it was the fact he wanted to spend a few more minutes bantering with Irelynn.

He'd always been a "list" man. So, in his mind, as he tamped in the post, he thought of the things that weren't so bad about Irelynn. She was a good mom to the twins, a woman who loved the Lord, was smart, responsible, and pretty.

Super pretty.

All right, so all of those things went in the left-hand column. Now for the not-so-pleasant attributes in the right-hand column: she defeated him at air hockey, was snobby when he first met her, and seemed odd about spending money for something so important as the remodel of the kids' rooms.

He again visualized the left-hand column, as he thought of how perfect she'd felt in his arms.

So maybe the left-hand column would win.

Maybe he'd spent far too much time with Isabelle getting this house thing under control, so Irelynn seemed like a refreshing reprieve.

Or maybe Quinton really was falling in love with her.

He unloaded his paint supplies and tapped on the door.

"Come in," she called from somewhere in the house.

He walked in and placed his supplies in Max's future room. "The mailbox is finished," he announced, meeting her in the kitchen.

Irelynn had placed a plate of cookies on the table. "They're still warm. Would you like some milk?"

"Sure. Are you going to join me?"

She shrugged and poured him a glass of milk. "I really should finish the website before Mom drops the twins off."

"Tell you what. If you're not finished by the time she gets here, I'll take the twins outside for a while to give you more time to finish."

Irelynn flashed him one of her smiles. Could he just sit there and bask in it all afternoon while eating cookies? "All right," she said slowly, taking a seat at the table.

Quinton sat across from Irelynn. The heap of chocolate crinkle cookies beckoned him. He took a bite and came to the realization that he would replace a million mailboxes just for one cookie. It melted in his mouth, and he reached for another. "These are delicious, Irelynn. They remind me of all the times Mom made homemade cookies for Nicole and me every Wednesday. She'd have a plate sitting on the table for us when we got home from school. I can't tell you the number of times I made myself sick eating cookies. It was worth it though." He paused. "I really miss my parents. They would have loved to have met Mia and Max."

"I'm sorry you've lost so many loved ones."

The concern in her voice touched him. Add that she was kindhearted to the list of favorable qualities in the left-hand column. "Thanks. I'm grateful I have the twins and Gram."

Irelynn appeared to want to say something. Was she thinking of her own parents? Maybe her dad? Had he passed away too? He wanted to ask. He should ask. Make conversation. "So, I know your mom, but does your dad live here too?"

She appeared taken aback by his question. Gram would probably tell him it wasn't gentlemanly to "pry."

"I don't know where he lives. He left Mom and me when I was five."

"Wow. I'm sorry, Irelynn."

"Thanks."

Did she want to say more? Should he pry?

He really did want to know more about her.

"The twins are lucky to have you, Quinton."

"They're pretty special to me."

With a saddened look that made him want to capture her in his arms all over again, Irelynn said, "I never knew the love of a dad."

How could Quinton answer that? He'd known the love of a dad. A godly man who put his family just under God in order of importance. "I'm sorry about that. Must have been tough."

"It was. Mom was amazing, though. She raised me single-handedly. There were times we didn't have much, but God always saw us through."

He put his hand on hers. It felt warm and soft beneath his calloused one.

They sat with no words between them while Quinton munched on his—what was it—his fifth cookie? But who was counting?

CHAPTER 19

*W*hy had she just shared all that with Quinton? Must be some secret ingredient in the cookies making her all sentimental. Still, while she saw a new, unexpected side of him, there was no reason he needed to know her deepest darkest secrets.

They had gotten along so well today after discussing the misunderstanding about what Troy said. After that mess was sorted out, they seemed to click with their banter. Totally unexpected. She hadn't wanted to speak one word to him after overhearing Troy's recommendation.

"You'll have to show me your website," Quinton said, interrupting her thoughts.

He wanted to see her website?

"Sure." Irelynn walked over to the desk with her computer. "It's for a health food store."

Quinton grabbed another cookie and stood to follow her. He peered over her shoulder at the computer screen. "Wow. That's impressive."

"I almost have it completed. It took me awhile to develop a color scheme. Here is the navigation bar." Irelynn put her mouse on the tabs at the top of the site. "Customers can shop online, contact the store with questions, and view health news and articles. I wanted to make it easy for the customer to find everything they needed in the most minimal amount of time."

"I should have you design a site for me."

"Really?"

"You'd think I'd have one by now, but I just haven't gotten around to it. Dad never saw the need, but..." Quinton shrugged. "Can I hire you to design one for Gregory Home Building and Remodeling?"

He wanted her to build a website for him? The Lord certainly answered her prayers in mysterious ways. Quinton Gregory of all people?

"Sure."

"Great. I'd like it to be user-friendly like this one with pictures of some of the houses I've built and some of the places I've remodeled."

"I--I can do that."

He grinned at her again. "I better get to painting and let you finish this website."

MOM ARRIVED 10 minutes later with Mia and Max. The two practically flew through the door and into the new rooms to see Quinton.

"Thank you so much for watching them, Mom. I was able to finish the health food store website."

"Glad to hear that. Did I see a new mailbox outside?"

"Yes, Quinton completely replaced the post and the mailbox."

"That was considerate of him."

"Hello, Mrs. Brady," said Quinton, walking from Mia's new room with a kid on each bicep.

"Quinton, hello. The mailbox looks nice."

He shot Irelynn a glance and grinned. "Irelynn promised me all the cookies I could eat if I'd fix it. I'd be a fool to pass up that kind of offer."

Mom arched an eyebrow. "Irelynn is an excellent baker."

"That she is."

Irelynn blushed. "Mia and Max, I missed you. Let's get you washed up so you can have a snack."

"Snack," reiterated Max, unclasping his hands from around Quinton's arm.

Mom followed Irelynn into the kitchen and whispered. "Is there something I'm missing here?"

"What do you mean?" Irelynn balanced Max on the counter and helped him wash his hands.

"You and Quinton seem to be getting along a lot better. You made him cookies, and he fixed your mailbox. Sounds serious. Should I put on some coffee?"

"Mom, I did not make *him* cookies. I had already mixed up the dough long before he arrived."

"Mmmmm." Mom tossed a sly grin Irelynn's way. "What happened to him being your nemesis?" She paused. "And what happened with the custody issue? Did you discuss it?"

"Yes. He says he has no intention of seeking full custody."

"And do you believe him?"

"Yes. I hope I'm not being too trusting, but I really do think he was being honest." Irelynn glanced around the corner into the children's new bedrooms to confirm Quinton was hard at work painting and not able to hear their conversation.

"I'm glad you believe him. You don't tend to trust people very easily, my dear." Mom placed an arm around Irelynn's shoulders.

Irelynn did have to admit Mom had a point. "I know. But I do believe him on this."

"I'm just glad you two are getting along better."

"It's what's best for the children, and the way Nicole wanted it."

Mom's expression indicated she didn't believe that any more than Irelynn did.

Who knew it would take a new mailbox and a batch of chocolate crinkle cookies for Irelynn to admit maybe she had been wrong about Quinton Gregory?

CHAPTER 20

*M*uch to Irelynn's surprise, Quinton arrived unexpectedly early the following morning dressed in workout clothes. His blue-and-gray tank top accentuated the muscle definition in his arms, and he toted a water bottle with his company's logo printed on it. "How about a morning run before I get started on the rooms?"

A morning run? Irelynn bemoaned the fact she felt sluggish and lethargic. But she would not turn down a run with Quinton no matter how early and unexpected. Not after their day yesterday.

Quinton smiled at her, a quirky smile she was really growing accustomed to, causing her heart to do a strange flip-flop in her chest.

Okay, so what was that about?

"With the warm weather, I figured today would be as good a day as any."

Irelynn pondered his enthusiastic attitude. When he moved down the street, would he want to run with her each morning?

She could grow accustomed to that.

"All right. Give me a few minutes to get the kids ready. They're still eating their cereal."

"Anything I can do to help?"

"Would you mind making sure the stroller tires aren't flat? I think I ran over a nail last time."

Last time. Her most recent run was right after she'd overheard Quinton's and Troy's conversation. Things had changed in such a short amount of time.

"Sure."

Mia and Max left the table and ran toward their uncle. He captured them in a hug.

"What do you think about Uncle Quinton going on a run with you and Aunt Irelynn today?"

"Can we go to the pwayground?" Mia asked.

"The pwayground," Max echoed.

"The playground sounds like an excellent idea. Finish up your breakfast, and I'll be right back."

Mia and Max squealed, their voices reaching high octaves. "Max, you get snacks. I'll get Baby," Mia commanded.

"Yes, me get snacks."

Irelynn watched the scene unfold. The mutual love and adoration between the three of them was evident. Something in her stomach clenched. *Please, Lord. Let Quinton and me raise Mia and Max in a way that honors You and makes Nicole proud.*

Moments later, the twins were seated in the stroller. "Need me to push the stroller?" Quinton asked.

"How about I push it on the way there and you push it on the way back?"

"Sounds fair to me." He took a swig of water and placed it in the mesh holder beneath where the children sat.

The fact he had the physique of a fit runner did not escape her attention.

Nerves overtook Irelynn. What if she couldn't keep up with Quinton's pace? What if her energy level never improved?

She needn't have worried. She started her fitness tracker and looped her hand through the black "emergency leash" to keep the stroller from getting too far ahead of her. Once her feet hit the path, the high of running took over, and Irelynn comfortably pushed the baby jogger. In her mind, there was nothing like an exhilarating run, especially when combined with a beautiful clear day and the sound of Mia's and Max's giggles intermingling with the random outside noises.

Quinton matched her pace, whether because that was the speed he was accustomed to running or he was being a gentleman.

She would never know, but she appreciated it.

QUINTON WAS surprised Irelynn agreed to allow him to run with her and the twins. He didn't want to take away that special moment they shared when they ran to the park, but he yearned to be a part of it.

Yearned to be a part of a family once again.

Irelynn's pace matched his, and Quinton found himself impressed. The woman was an experienced runner, especially while maneuvering the baby jogger. Every so often, she'd ask the kids a question, then laugh at their responses. Quinton could see she loved them.

Nicole had made the right choice.

Not that Quinton would have admitted that when he'd first heard the details of the custody arrangement.

Irelynn had fixed her hair into a long smooth ponytail that swished back and forth as she ran. She sported a burgundy-colored tank top with the words, "Run...then coffee" plastered on the front. To say he was attracted to her was an understatement.

They continued down Third Avenue when he saw a familiar black SUV. The words *Isabelle Vacura, Real Estate Agent. Don't hire me unless you want the best.* were emblazoned on the windows in bright lettering.

Quinton turned his head just in time to see Isabelle craning her neck out the window. Was she attempting to get a better look at him and Irelynn? Isabelle lowered her dark sunglasses and stared. Quinton raised a hand to wave.

Isabelle didn't wave, but continued on her route, her head still hanging out the window. Quinton was surprised she wasn't concerned about the wind messing up her hair.

A glance over at Irelynn told him she hadn't seen Isabelle watching them. Who knew what Isabelle was thinking as she drove by them. Quinton didn't care, other than he wanted nothing to jeopardize the closing, which was still a few weeks away.

Irelynn rounded the corner following the path, and entered the park area. Mia and Max began clapping. "There's the pwayground!" exclaimed Mia.

"The pwayground," agreed Max.

Quinton loved those two kids. He only hoped he could do right by them, not like what he'd done when entrusted with their father's life.

Irelynn parked the stroller and unlatched the harness belts. Mia and Max lurched forward and out of the stroller. "Ready to spend some time at the playground?" she asked, pushing the button to stop her fitness tracker.

"As long as I don't have to go down the slide, I'm up for it."

Irelynn laughed. "Just to warn you, they may ask you to do just that. Last time we were here, I tried the swings, the slide, and the chicken on the springs that goes forward and backward. Let me tell you, I slept well that night."

He liked her laugh. It was pleasing to hear, not all high-pitched and dramatic like Isabelle's.

So, why was he comparing her to Isabelle? There really was no comparison. Isabelle couldn't hold a candle to Irelynn, even when Irelynn was at her worst.

Quinton followed Irelynn to the swings, where she stood behind the children, giving them gentle pushes. "Actually, the chicken looks fun. Can it safely hold our weight? Maybe you could try that again, and I'll try the turtle right next to it."

"At first, I wasn't sure. But then I found a weight limit sticker on the bottom of the chicken, and it said it could accommodate up to 200 pounds. I guess the manufacturer realized parents would play on it too."

"That's reassuring. I'm about 20 pounds under that, so it should work."

Moments later, Quinton and Irelynn followed the twins to the area where the springy chicken and turtle stood mounted in the wood chips. "You ready for this?" Quinton asked. He winked at Max. "I'm going to ride the turtle and Aunt Irelynn is going to try the chicken again."

Max giggled and pointed at the turtle. Quinton climbed on the toy and let it spring all the way forward, taking him almost to a turtle nose-dive in the wood chips. Irelynn did the same on the chicken.

"These are actually kind of fun," Quinton admitted.

"Not too bad if you like the forward and back motion," answered Irelynn. "Although if I stay on too long, I tend to get motion sickness." She paused. "Oh, I almost forgot to tell you..."

Quinton propelled himself forward again. "What's that?"

"Mrs. Caruthers saw a man walking around your new house. Apparently, whenever someone new moves into the neighborhood, it causes her concern. She found her husband's antique binoculars and peered through them for a better glimpse. She drew a sketch of the man and the man's truck—or should I say the rear portion of the truck, since that's all she could see. Something about her being a forensic artist or something."

"Mrs. Caruthers, a forensic artist?"

"Something to that effect. Anyway, she showed me her sketches." Irelynn giggled. "That woman is a card. The sketch of the man was a stick-figure and she had shaded in the drawing of the truck." Irelynn paused. "Come to think of it, maybe it was you that she was depicting in her sketch."

"Are you sure it was supposed to be me? Maybe it was someone else looking at the house."

Irelynn shook her head. "There was a strong resemblance between you and the sketch. Something about the hair was similar."

"The hair?"

They both started laughing then, their amusement chorusing throughout the play area. "Really. You should see her drawings. They are in no way forensic artist material."

"Glad you think her sketch resembled me. I wouldn't want anyone else setting their sights on that luxury home I'm planning to remodel."

"No, probably not a lot of competition. Not yet. But after the owner of Gregory Home Building and Remodeling works his magic, it'll be the nicest house in the neighborhood."

Irelynn's confidence in him provided just the encouragement he needed to make a go of restoring the unkempt house. "Thanks. I hope so. It'll take some work, but it'll be worth it."

"You have talent, Quinton."

His eyes met hers and all commotion around them became background noise. The carefree moment further enhanced the growing connection between them.

A tug on his arm interrupted Quinton's focus. "You are way too big for that," Mia said, hands on her hips. "It's for little kids."

"The slide," said Max, pointing at the slide.

"He wants you to go on the Curly."

Quinton looked from Mia to Max. He did not want to go down the slide. He'd never much cared for slides, especially not enclosed curly ones. "I think I'll stay here." Quinton took a peek at Irelynn. Her ponytail swung with her momentum on the toy and her sunglasses fell on her nose, as if they were reading glasses. *Man, she's cute.*

Mia stood by him and reached for his hand. "Come on, Uncle Quinton. Let's go on the Curly."

"All right." Quinton relented. He'd do just about anything for his niece, even take on the daredevil task of going down the slide. Besides, he wanted Irelynn to think he was a doting uncle.

Quinton stood and followed the twins. "You two go first," he suggested, eyeing the green enclosed playground toy.

Max nodded and climbed up the stairs and plopped into the slide.

"I thought you said you weren't going to attempt the Curly," said Irelynn standing next to him.

"I'm a pushover."

"Seems that way." She gave him a playful jab.

He liked it when they playfully bantered back and forth.

"Your turn," said Mia, after sliding down the slide.

Quinton gingerly climbed the seven stairs to the top of the slide. Sitting down, he edged into the opening of the slide and pushed off the sides. Midway through, something traumatic happened.

He became wedged. Quinton turned one way, then the other, but his body, or rather, his shoulders, wouldn't budge. Why hadn't he thought about that before he decided to show off in front of Irelynn and declare himself Uncle of the Year?

Quinton could hear the three laughing outside the slide. They probably figured he was joking and would come out the bottom of the slide any minute.

A thought struck him. How much could the slide hold? Was there a weight limit on it like there was the springy toys? He hoped he was within those limits. It wouldn't do his back any favors to crash through the thin plastic.

He'd dodged enemy bombs, survived killer heat in Afghanistan, lived in a constant state of heightened awareness at what the terrorists might plot next, but this business of being stuck in a slide...

"Quinton, are you all right in there?"

Irelynn's voice.

He thought she'd never ask.

Quinton turned from one side to the other, again attempting to dislodge himself. He even dug his heels into the slide to attempt to get some momentum to propel himself downward, to no avail. The slide shook, but his body remained where it was.

"Guess I'm stuck in here, Irelynn," he called. *Fortunately, it isn't any hotter outside yet. A guy could die from suffocation in this inferno.*

"Really?"

Quinton heard her laugh.

"Yes, really." He noticed the edge in his voice as it echoed. Why would he joke about being stuck in the slide? No man in their right mind would have attempted this feat, especially without checking the dimensions first.

And I build houses for a living?

"Can you wiggle and try to get yourself out?"

"I've tried it, but it's not working." Sweat poured down his forehead and his legs stuck to the plastic.

"Is Uncle Quinton okay?" Mia asked.

A sound like a muffled sniffle came through the bottom opening of the slide. "Uncle Quinton?"

"I'm okay, Max."

If he didn't have a heatstroke or panic attack first.

"Uh, look, Irelynn, I hate to admit this, but..."

"You're truly stuck."

"Yep."

"All right. I'll call the fire department."

Great. As long as it wasn't in *The Chokecherry Heights Gazette*, Quinton could live with the fire department rescuing him.

He blew a deep breath and shifted again. The slide groaned. Maybe if he tried again...after all, hadn't he wiggled through tunnels and ditches during his training?

Never mind the fact he was claustrophobic.

He heard Irelynn's voice. "Yes, he is stuck in the slide at Chokecherry Heights Park off of Whitmore Street."

What Quinton wouldn't do for a swig of water about now. As if she'd heard his thoughts, Mia's voice sounded at the top of the slide. "Are you thirsty, Uncle Quinton?"

"Yes."

"Okay."

Within seconds, a loud clinking noise could be heard. His water bottle then plunked him in the head.

"I rowed it to you," Mia called.

Sad thing was, there was no way he could maneuver himself to take a drink. Instead, the water bottle rested on the top of his head.

It sounded like Irelynn had clicked off her call. "The fire department is on their way," she said.

"Thanks."

"Quinton, are you all right?"

The concern in her voice did something strange to him. He liked it that she cared. "Yeah, I will be."

A disturbing thought entered Quinton's mind.

Once word got out about his rescue, he would never hear the end of this.

IRELYNN NOTICED the only thing bruised on Quinton was his ego. He'd known two of the firemen who'd rescued him. They had minced no words ribbing him for getting stuck.

"Didn't you realize you were wider than the slide?" one fireman asked.

Poor guy. He'd likely hear about his adventure in the Curly for years to come.

The firemen left after Quinton assured them three times they did not need to call for medical help.

Quinton limped. "Okay if we walk back?" he asked, reaching over to push the baby jogger.

"Absolutely. And I'm going to push the stroller."

"If you're sure?"

"I'm 100 percent sure."

Quinton nodded and placed a hand on his lower back. "Remind me to never again attempt to slide down the Curly."

She tossed him a sympathetic glance. "I will. And for what it's worth, you did create a memory for the kids today. A wonderful memory."

"I guess it was worth it then, huh?"

And worth it to spend more time with him, since her feelings had slowly begun to change. Although Irelynn didn't say so.

For these new feelings for him had taken her by surprise.

CHAPTER 21

Quinton joined Gram at the gazebo behind the Chokecherry Heights Assisted Living Home. "I ordered us some sweet tea," Gram announced, as Quinton took a seat across from her. He grinned at Gram. If there was one thing his Southern grandma loved, it was her tea.

"How has your week been?" Quinton asked, taking a drink of the cold beverage.

"Lively so far. I'm in the running for the top spot in the bridge tournament. It's my second favorite game after Uno."

"Congratulations, Gram. I always knew you had a knack for being a celebrity."

Gram's face glowed, and her blue eyes sparkled. "I won't tell you about the competition or lack thereof." She paused. "Are y'all fully recovered from getting stuck in that playground slide?"

"Barely." He grinned. "It was an adventure, and one I'm sure I'll never hear the end of from Irelynn and the twins, and especially my friends at the fire department."

"Who knew such an atrocity could happen? At a playground, no less."

Quinton reveled in Gram's dramatic teasing. "At least the slide didn't collapse."

Gram's giggle filled the sunny afternoon. "For that we are grateful." Her tone turned serious. "Have you learned your lesson, young man?"

"I have. No more slides for me."

"That's probably wise. So, did you close on the house yet?"

"Within the next two months."

"Now, you know I have to say this...are you sure you aren't getting in over your heard with this mortgage?"

Quinton appreciated Gram's concern more than she knew. "No, it's all good. I plan to do the extensive remodeling myself as I can between my jobs, so that'll save me a lot of money. Basically, I will just have to pay for materials. I spoke with the bank and was able to take out a loan for an increased amount to cover those expenses."

"As long as you have it all under control."

"I do. Don't worry, Gram."

"Pshaw, you know I do. I know how much this house means to you so you can live closer to Irelynn." A flicker of mischievousness in Gram's eyes at the mention of Irelynn's name did not sit well with Quinton.

He braced himself for what was to come. "It's for ease of the custody arrangement of the twins."

"Ahhh." The mischievousness remained.

"Gram..."

"I just think she's an awful nice gal and one you ought to think about courting."

Quinton chuckled at Gram's antiquated terminology. "I'm not in the market to be dating since I have a lot on my plate at the moment. Between Mia and Max and owning my own business, who has time?"

"You could make time. The twins adore Irelynn, and she is

such a lovely young woman. I enjoy chatting with her at church each Sunday. You do have to admit she's pretty."

Pretty didn't begin to cover it.

"You haven't spoken about how she irritates you quite as much during your past couple of visits."

Very astute, Gram. "Yeah, well, we have been getting along a lot better."

"Good for you, although I assume it's for Nicole's sake."

Gram, you know me too well. "We've come to an understanding."

"Is that a good thing?"

A really good thing. "I realized she's not as bad as I thought she was." As soon as the words slipped out, Quinton regretted them.

"Oooh. As they say, that is how it all starts. With your grandpa and I—when I realized he wasn't as bad as I originally thought— let's just say it wasn't long before wedding bells were chiming."

"No wedding bells here, Gram." Although the thought didn't horrify him like it once had.

Whoa. Slow down. Just because you're getting along doesn't mean you and Irelynn will be meeting at the altar and be the next Gram and Gramps clones. Far from it.

"Nicole always wanted the two of you to court. As do I. Maybe I'll ask for that for Christmas."

Had Gramps realized Gram's slightly manipulative side? Likely so in all those years of marriage. Quinton needed to change the subject.

Fast.

"Mia and Max have been doing better with getting adjusted to all the changes."

"Now that's an answer to prayer. It's rough on young ones to lose their parents." Gram appeared thoughtful. "When I lost Daddy as a child, it was tough." She cleared her throat. "Now tell me, Quinton, how are you doing with your PTSD?"

"Better. The support group I attend is helping, and I've had several meetings with our pastor about Tom."

Gram patted him on the arm. "You're right to seek help. You've been through a lot and seen a lot. There's no shame in needing assistance."

"It took me awhile to see that. Pride, I guess."

"Absolutely. None of us want to admit when we need help. I'm praying for healing for you and that you won't be so hard on yourself over Tom's death."

"That'll take some time, Gram. Even the therapist said that." Quinton swallowed hard. Gram was the only one, besides those in the support group and Pastor, who knew about his struggle with guilt. "That's why I can't fail Nicole in the raising of the twins."

"You won't fail. Not with God guiding you. But, yes, I know what you mean. You're doing a fine a job, and I couldn't be prouder of you." Gram's eyes lit with tears. "Now then, you just need to find a sweet wife to assist you with this important role. Someone who loves Mia and Max and will raise them for the Lord. And yes, before you ask, I'm hinting."

Was that why Irelynn's face suddenly appeared in Quinton's mind? He attempted to shove it away. Yes, he was falling in love with her, but marriage? "Marriage isn't in the plans at the moment, Gram." How did they get back to this topic?

"I know, I know. But when the time does come, it ought to be a woman who loves the Lord, loves the twins, and someone you enjoy being with. Someone you have much in common with."

Quinton tried to interrupt Gram and talk about anything but marriage. Sweet tea? The cows in the distance? The weather?

But Gram didn't allow his interruption. Her face took on the "I'm going to give you a lecture, now please pay attention" look. She held up a finger. "I'm not saying you'll find someone perfect, because you won't. But you will find someone perfect *for you*. Your grandfather, God rest his precious soul, had a way of getting on my nerves at times. Oh, and to be sure, I got on his. But we loved each other something fierce. We had a lot in common, even though I'd never cottoned to woodworking. I'd cut off my finger before I could use even one of those table saws, but we had much we liked to do together. Strolls in the evenings down the country road, attending church potlucks, and playing a fiercely competitive game of Uno in our later years."

Irelynn's face again flashed in Quinton's mind. Air hockey. Running. Pizza. Ice cream. Homemade cookies at the table. Her in his arms. He blinked and willed a picture of the latest power tool at Nathanson's to replace any stray romantic notions floating through his mind.

Didn't happen.

"Now then," Gram continued. "You two put the Lord first in your marriage and everything else will fall into place."

"Marriage isn't on the radar, Gram."

"When it is."

"It won't be."

"Such a stubborn young man. All right, I'll quit pestering you about it this time. I don't want you to take on the notion visiting Gram is unpleasant."

Quinton chuckled. He could never think that. He loved Gram, even if she was overbearing in her quest to see him married, which would never happen, not even with his recent feelings for Irelynn. Quinton was content with his life just the way it was—as a single man.

"Oh, look, there's Karla," Gram said, nodding toward a young woman pushing an elderly man in a wheelchair.

Quinton waved at Karla Eisle, as she pushed the wheelchair toward the gazebo. "Quinton, how are you today?"

"Doing good. Karla, you remember my grandma, Mrs. Gregory?"

"Yes, a pleasure to see you again. And you both remember my grandfather, Frederick Eisle?"

Quinton reached a hand toward Mr. Eisle. "Nice to see you again."

"I finally connected with Irelynn Brady, the web designer you referred to me. She's all set to create my website. I can't wait to see the finished product."

"She does an excellent job," Quinton answered. He'd known Karla since their school days, even though she and her fiancé were both several years older than Quinton.

"I have a feeling I'll be quite pleased. We'll be off now, but it's good to see you both."

Quinton and Gram waved as Karla and Mr. Eisle continued down the sidewalk. Add another entry into the left-hand column for Irelynn.

The woman could really build a website.

Funny how that left-hand side far outweighed the right.

CHAPTER 22

The ride to Nathanson's was filled with anticipation. Today would be the day they would choose the flooring for the remodel. Only mouldings and finishing touches remained, and Mia and Max could move into their new rooms.

"I want a pink floor," chirped Mia.

Max shook his head. "No pink. I want twains."

Quinton chuckled. "We have ourselves some opinionated children when it comes to flooring."

Irelynn rested her arm on the console between she and Quinton. Hearing him say "we" warmed her heart. They were becoming a family, albeit an unconventional one, and the cohesiveness between she and Quinton had strengthened considerably in recent days.

"And I want a pink ceiling like my walls. Pink everything."

"How about some other colors too, Mia?" Irelynn asked.

"No, only pink. Pink is my fwavorite color."

They stopped at the stoplight and Quinton placed his hand on hers, triggering an electrical jolt up her arm. The wordless communication between them when their eyes connected said more than words ever could.

178

Did she dare to believe this was the beginning of something more than just friendship?

And dare she hope?

Could Mom and Nicole both have been right about her and Quinton?

The stoplight changed to green, and Quinton returned his attention to the road, but his hand remained on hers. The naturalness of it lent to the real possibility she was growing fond of this man who had stepped into her life in the most unorthodox way.

QUINTON LOADED the twins into the shopping cart. As they strode toward the front door, he caught their reflections in the window. To the unknowing observer, they would appear to be just like any other family on a mission to find the right flooring for their children's rooms.

The thought took him back to the many times his own family, which included the same familial dynamics of a dad, mom, daughter, and son, would shop at the store. Grief over the loss of his parents who would never know Mia and Max and over the loss of Nicole who would never see her children grow up clouded his mind.

But the thought of carrying on the Gregory tradition with the next generation competed with those thoughts. The past was painful, but the promise of raising Mia and Max helped ease that pain.

And with Irelynn as his comrade, the future looked hopeful.

Irelynn. She had stolen his heart in a short amount of time, something he never anticipated would happen.

The aroma of carpeting, vinyl, and laminate greeted them as they entered the flooring section. "Are you thinking of carpet or another flooring alternative?" he asked Irelynn.

"I can see pros and cons to both, but I actually was thinking of going more the laminate route."

"They're having a sale on certain brands of laminate this week." Quinton led them to a display of an assortment of colors and textures. Irelynn stepped forward and inspected the tag depicting various features and prices of the laminate.

"Is this a quality one?" she asked, pointing to one of the lesser-expensive choices.

Quinton examined the flooring. "It'll do, but this one is a step up." He pointed to a similar sample on the display rack. "It's only about $4 more a case. Would that work for your budget?"

Irelynn appeared to be debating his question. Was money a concern? That thought hadn't crossed his mind when they had opened up a charge account for her or with the purchases he'd made for the remodel, but it made sense that it could be. "How about we go with the better-quality flooring and I'll put the difference on my tab."

She pressed her lips together, as if contemplating his words. "If you're sure."

"I'm sure. It's going to take a lot of abuse from the kids and their toys, so we might as well get them something that will last."

Her shoulders relaxed. "All right. That sounds good."

They chose a warm pale brown color, and Quinton placed several boxes of the laminate and the underlayment into the cart. "I think we'll be pleased with this choice."

"My twains!" exclaimed Max, pointing a finger toward a brightly-colored children's area rug with trains and a train track on it. He wiggled in the cart and craned his neck to get a better view.

"Since we're going laminate, Max could have his train track," suggested Quinton, pushing the cart toward the throw rug.

"And my pink floor," said Mia, her eyes scoping out a bright fuzzy pink area rug.

Irelynn laughed. "I think it's settled. Laminate flooring with area rugs."

He would retrieve the throw rugs later on his own tab.

While the twins needed their rooms completed, he would miss being at Irelynn's house for more than kid pickup/return. His work load for the next few weeks would be insane, and he would need to be mindful to carve out time for the twins and Irelynn.

CHAPTER 23

Irelynn sat next to Quinton at Carlos's wedding two weeks later. She did her best to hold back tears a she watched Carlos and Chandra look lovingly into each other's eyes. She'd been to a few weddings in her time, but none exhibiting the display of love as this one did.

And she didn't even know the bride and groom.

Irelynn snuck a peek at Quinton. He had dressed up for the occasion with a blue-and-white checked button-up plaid shirt. If she hadn't thought he was good-looking before, she did now.

Had Irelynn really hoped Quinton would forget Carlos had invited them to his wedding that day at Nathanson's? That seemed like forever ago now.

The unexpected had become a reality.

"You look beautiful today," Quinton whispered in her ear.

The words came out of nowhere, and when she turned to thank him, his face was close to hers. So close. She could smell his aftershave, and she inhaled the increasingly recognizable scent.

"So do you," Irelynn whispered back.

Quinton's face held a peculiar expression, and that's when

Irelynn realized her insane statement. "I mean, you don't look beautiful, but..."

"SSSHHH!" an elderly woman in the row in front of them hissed, as she glared at them over her shoulder.

"Sorry," Irelynn mouthed.

She focused her attention once again to the bride and groom. Chandra's white dress flowed with a long train, carried by two adorable little girls. Her reddish hair was curled in ringlets, and her face glowed.

Carlos resembled every bit the polished groom with his white tuxedo.

What would it be like to have found true love, as it appeared Carlos and Chandra had?

Irelynn lacked the luxury of having an example to follow in that arena. Her earliest memories consisted of her parents fighting, her dad being cruel and unkind, and then permanently leaving. Mom had never found anyone else to take on the role of her husband and a father to Irelynn.

Quinton faced her, and their eyes connected. He flashed her one of his smiles that made her blush. Knowing the red crept up her face, Irelynn diverted her eyes to her lap. Their hands were close and she longed for him to reach over and hold her hand.

She inwardly chuckled at the thought.

This was Quinton Gregory, after all.

But not the same Quinton Gregory she'd once known. Not the one who rated low on the chart of friendship and high on the chart of nemesis.

No, this was a man she'd developed feelings for over the past couple of weeks, much to her surprise. She could try to deny it, but it wouldn't do any good. He filled her thoughts more often now, and she saw him less.

Especially with the remodel being complete and the twins' belongings moved into their respective rooms.

Did he feel the same about her?

~

"THIS IS MY FRIEND, IRELYNN BRADY," Quinton said to a group of his friends from high school. Would he someday be introducing her as his girlfriend? The more time he spent with her, the more Quinton was beginning to think of her as more than a friend. The thought struck him out of nowhere. Sure, she was compassionate, thoughtful, and smart, and he wasn't sure why he'd ever considered her his enemy. But he wasn't even sure she felt the same.

He thought of his own parents' marriage. Could he even ever hope to have something close to what they had shared before the Lord took them home?

He had this urge to reach for her hand. To tell her again how beautiful she looked. To dance with her to the music that played through the sound system. To get to know her better. To make plans *with* her for Mia's and Max's future.

Quinton led her to the receiving line. Carlos emitted a huge grin, obviously proud of his new bride. The last thing on Quinton's mind was marriage, especially since he had to focus his attention on his two most critical responsibilities: raising the twins and rehabbing the family business. After his return from Afghanistan, his commitments had transformed into unexpected chaos at times.

But thinking about Carlos starting a new life with the woman he loved...

Knock it off, man. You're getting all soft and mushy.

Besides, some things he just couldn't do for Nicole. Like get married.

"Congratulations, Carlos and Chandra," Quinton said, offering a firm handshake to Carlos.

"Thanks."

"Chandra, this is my friend, Irelynn." The two women greeted each other and seemed to hit it off. Or maybe it was that a woman could always find something to chat about with another woman.

"You two are next," Carlos winked at Quinton.

"None of that marriage stuff for me, but we're happy for you guys."

"Yes, you two really make a charming couple," chimed in Chandra.

Irelynn shook her head. "We're just friends."

"Sure, that's what Carlos and I used to say...at first." Chandra planted a kiss on Carlos's plump cheek.

Quinton ushered them through the line of attendants. Yes, he and Irelynn were just friends. And that was so much better than the rivals they were in the not-so-distant past.

But did friends have the feelings for each other that he was beginning to have for Irelynn?

QUINTON LED her to the porch. "I had a good time tonight."

"Me too."

They stood there in the same awkward silence they always did. Wondering what to say. How to act. What to think.

"It was a nice wedding," she finally said. "Carlos and Chandra seem really nice."

"They are. I don't know Chandra well, but Carlos and I go way back. I think he secretly had a crush on Chandra even in high school."

"Wow. That's a neat love story."

"Yeah."

More silence.

Irelynn stole a hurried glimpse toward the house. Mom was watching the twins and all the lights were on, lighting up the entire neighborhood. She spied Mrs. Caruthers's house, thankful the eccentric woman wasn't outside taking notes.

"I should probably go. Do you think the kids are still up?"

The eagerness in his eyes told her he likely wanted to tell them good night before he left. "I doubt it. Mom is pretty good about getting them to bed on time. I'm still working on those bedtime battles."

"I hear you there. Must come with experience."

"It must."

Quinton took a step toward her. Irelynn's feet remained locked in place. Would he kiss her? Did she want him to kiss her?

Yes. Yes, she did.

Her heart pounded in her chest.

He reached a hand toward her face and caressed her cheek. "Good night, Irelynn." His voice was low, barely above a whisper.

She blinked. Was this what it was like to fall in love? "Good night, Quinton."

There was a look in his eyes she couldn't ascertain. Did he have feelings for her, as she did for him? It would appear so.

Too soon, Quinton shoved his hands in his pockets. "I'll see you tomorrow morning for our run before I head to work."

She looked forward to another run with him. "Just so you don't get stuck in the slide again."

Quinton chuckled. She really liked his laugh. Really liked him.

When had all that happened? During their time at The Pizza Slice? The ice cream stand date? Their run to the park?

"I'm not going down that road—or should I say slide—again."

She laughed in response, taking in his attractive appearance one last time before he left.

"Well, good night." He said again. He stepped off the porch, pausing to wave before heading toward his truck.

Leaving Irelynn with a heartbeat that rivaled when she was running at her top speed.

And a twinge of disappointment that he hadn't kissed her.

Mom met her at the door. "How did it go?"

"It was a lovely wedding."

"You and Quinton seem to be getting along so much better."

"Mom..."

"Could it be this topic might get serious? I could put on some coffee."

Irelynn giggled. "It's much too late for coffee, Mom. You and I both know we wouldn't sleep a wink of we drank any tonight."

"True. So I saw him walk you to the porch." Mom's face shone as though she was a little girl awaiting her next Christmas gift.

"Yes, you were right. He is a gentleman."

"So maybe he's not your nemesis anymore?"

Something like that. "I suppose you could say we're friends."

Mom's Cheshire grin did not put Irelynn at ease. "Do tell."

"Okay, I do like him. Sort of. He's nicer than I first thought and he does an incredible job with the twins, and he's attractive and all that..."

"I'll resist the urge to tell you 'I told you so.'"

"Thanks for the grace, Mom."

"Anytime. By the way, Mia and Max were well-behaved. We did some crafts, and they can't wait to show you their creations."

"Thank you for watching them for me."

"You're welcome."

"Oh, and Mom?"

"Yes?"

"Did I see you casting a glance in Mr. Wilson's direction last Sunday?"

Mom's face turned bright red. Must have been where Irelynn inherited her insta-blush tendencies. "I need to go since I have to go to work early tomorrow."

"He does seem like a pleasant fellow. Overly gregarious, but pleasant."

"I suppose you could say we're friends."

"Where have I heard that before?"

Mom grabbed her purse. "I really must go."

"Sure, a speedy exit to avoid an interrogation. See, Mom, I learned from the best."

"He's a friend. That's all."

"Well, all I can say is we need to find out his first name and he has to go through strict and thorough background checks. Oh, and provide 15 letters of reference before I can even allow him to date my mom."

"Who said anything about dating? Or are you considering dating Quinton?"

"Mom, you're the master at changing subjects."

"And you're the master at avoiding them."

They both laughed then, and Irelynn reveled in their camaraderie.

THAT EVENING AFTER MOM LEFT, Irelynn was too keyed up to sleep. The night's events rammed through her mind on auto-replay.

She sat on her front porch and gazed up at the stars. This was her quiet time. Time to spend in prayer, and time reflecting on what it was God was trying to teach her—and had recently taught her—through the trials she'd been through.

Gratitude filled her heart. For Mom. For the twins. For more work to ease her financial burden. For Quinton.

Yes, she thanked the Lord for Quinton.

Did the Lord have further plans where he was concerned?

CHAPTER 24

Irelynn watched the clock in anticipation for Quinton's arrival for their morning run. Something had definitely changed in the way she felt about him. She wished for more remodeling projects on her house just to see him more often. He'd been overly busy with all of his work projects, and with the exception of seeing him when they exchanged the children, in church, and at the wedding, Irelynn hadn't seen nearly as much of Quinton as she would have liked in recent days.

Mia and Max were having struggles today with bickering, tantrums, and disobedience. It would benefit them all to experience some time in the fresh air. "Mia, Max, please pick up your toys before Uncle Quinton gets here."

She then scrambled to ready herself. Pulling on her favorite burgundy tank top and running shorts, Irelynn then wrapped the matching hair tie around her thick hair and tugged it into a high ponytail. She added some mascara, eye shadow, and a light dusting of coverup. If someone had asked her weeks before if she cared about her appearance before Quinton's arrival, she would have answered with an astounding "no."

But things had changed.

She couldn't wait to see him.

A knock on the door told Irelynn he'd arrived. She rushed to the front door, mindful of the trail of toys the twins were supposedly working on returning to their bedrooms, and unlocked the door.

Quinton stood on the other side, two water bottles in hand. "I thought you might like this," he said, handing her a sleek new water bottle with his company's logo printed on the side.

"Thank you." How had she not realized in those early days how considerate Quinton was?

They stood there opposite from each other, and Irelynn wished she could fly into his strong arms.

What a crazy notion. As if you're in some romance novel or movie.

Instead, the twins rushed toward their uncle and greeted him with their traditional hug, so characteristic of their relationship with him.

"I'll go fill this up, and then we should be ready."

"How's today going?" Quinton asked when she returned from filling her water bottle.

"The twins are having a challenging day."

"Sorry to hear that. Anything I can do to help?"

Irelynn appreciated his thoughtfulness. "I think just getting out will help a lot. They are extremely unruly today, not to mention bickering and tantrums." She paused. "How is your day going?"

"Crazy busy. We've just about finished the one Waterbury Acres house, which is a good thing since next week is the deadline."

Irelynn wasn't watching where she was going then. She didn't see Max's latest building block creation in the middle of the floor. And she couldn't anticipate what would happen next.

In a matter of milliseconds, she went from an upright position to a stumbling, bumbling, clumsy ballerina, as her feet connected with the creation.

"Whoa, there!"

In an instant, she was captured in strong arms, safe from crashing into an oafish lump on the floor.

Quinton's arms wrapped around her tight, and she could hear the thrumming of her heartbeat—or was it his—in her ears.

"You okay?"

She glanced up into Quinton's eyes. Her knight in shining armor. "I--I think I'm okay." Her words came out in a breathless gasp.

He held her there, and she willed for him to do so for far longer than a few minutes. His arms felt safe, and not only from the dangerous floor below. It was like she belonged there, secure in his embrace. "I told the kids to clean up their toys." This time her voice came out a whisper.

Quinton leaned his head toward hers and brushed her lips with his. His lips were warm against hers as the slight touch became a full kiss. Her heart raced and all else was temporarily forgotten.

It had all the makings of a fairy tale when a scream erupted, interrupting the romantic moment.

"YOU BROKE MY BABY!"

The moment lost, Irelynn turned her head around to see a sobbing Mia clutching Baby and Max sneering at his sister.

"What happened?" she asked, disappointed at the inter-ruption.

"Max—he broke Baby. She only has one arm now."

"Your fault, Mia," snapped Max.

"Was not."

"Was too."

Within a split second, Mia picked up another toy from the floor and wacked Max with it.

"Owww," Max whined.

"You should never hurt Baby." Mia cradled her doll in her arms. "She'll never be the same."

Quinton stepped in and began the reprimanding, while Irelynn searched her brain for a way she could reattach the "broken arm."

"But, Uncle Quinton, it's Max's fault."

Quinton kneeled to the height of the twins and looked them both in the eye. "Max, you shouldn't have hurt Baby, and Mia, it was not all right to hit Max."

"But I loved Baby all my life and now she's hurted." Her lip quivered.

"We can send Baby to the dolly hospital, Mia, but you two are in big trouble," interjected Irelynn.

"Big twubble," copied Max, pointing a stubby finger at his sister.

"Both of you, Max," said Quinton.

Irelynn observed, thankful Quinton had taken over this round of discipline. Being a parent was tough, but at least she had an ally in the process.

QUINTON TOOK A DEEP BREATH. "I'm not sure I'm equipped to do this." He paused. "The bickering and the broken baby dolls."

Irelynn gaze held his. "Me either." She giggled, a soft, captivating laugh.

How could something so right as her in his arms, be interrupted by something so asinine as two toddlers in a squabble? He longed to hold her again. Kiss her fully. Tell her how he'd come to feel for her.

"God has a sense of humor giving us two rambunctious children. How can we not laugh and see the humor in it all?"

"Gram would say He knows what He's doing."

"And that He walks with us through whatever He allows to happen in our lives."

Quinton nodded. "I, for one, need that."

"Me too."

Should he take Irelynn in his arms again? Finish where they left off? He took a step toward her and reached for her hands. "Glad we're in this together."

"Yes, those two need us."

"Is it too early for them to take naps?" His gaze darted toward the clock. It was 8:00 a.m. "Maybe a nap would improve their behavior."

"They've only been up about an hour, so it's probably too soon."

Quinton thought of how perfect her hands felt in his. Just like how perfect she felt in his arms.

"If only adults could take naps whenever we have meltdowns," mused Irelynn.

"And have a pair of footy pajamas."

"Then our lives would be perfect."

He released her hands and took a strand of her hair between his fingers. He loved her hair. He leaned in and kissed the strand that he held.

Quinton didn't have to plan on his next move. It would be automatic the second his lips found hers. A full kiss this time.

But it wasn't to happen. His phone rang, interrupting the moment.

Unfortunately, he had to take this call.

"I'm sorry," he said, as he clicked on the phone. Just as Quinton thought. "I have a situation at the Waterbury Acres house."

"All right."

He noticed the disappointment spreading across her face. "I'm sorry, Irelynn. Can I make this up to you?"

"How about tomorrow?"

"Tomorrow early afternoon, I have to meet the concrete guy at my house, but after that?"

"Sounds good." She tossed him a smile he couldn't resist.

"It's a date then."

Tomorrow couldn't come soon enough.

CHAPTER 25

Irelynn received a Nathanson's bill in the mail the following morning. Even with the consistent monthly payments, she still had a long way to go before paying off the remodeling supplies, but at least she was getting closer, laminate flooring notwithstanding.

She perused the bill, searching for the mailbox, post, and area rugs. However, the most recent charge was the laminate from several days ago.

Had Quinton purchased the mailbox, post, and area rugs on his account?

One more reason to like him.

She decided to bake him homemade cookies for their running date in response to his generous gesture. "Should we make Uncle Quinton some cookies?"

"Oh, yes. He *loves* cookies," declared Mia.

"And cookies for Max," said Max, licking his lips.

Grateful that broken babies and retaliatory hits were forgotten for the time being, Irelynn rummaged through the cupboards to see if she had all the ingredients she'd need. Unfortunately, she was out of flour and eggs. If she was efficient, she could go to the store and be back before making lunch for two growing children.

An hour later, she pushed a cart with a squeaky wheel at Shifflett's Grocery and Deli. Mia sat in the front part of the cart, while Max sat in the basket. Irelynn whizzed around the corners, grocery list in hand. Hopefully she wouldn't see anyone she knew since she hadn't taken the time to change from her jeans and t-shirt with the orange-and-yellow stain on it from making homemade crafting clay with the twins.

After retrieving the eggs, Irelynn made a beeline for the baking aisle for the flour and chocolate chips.

"Fancy seeing you here."

Irelynn whipped around to see none other than Isabelle Vacura reaching for a pizza crust mix.

"Hello, Ms. Vacura."

"Oh, please. Call me Isabelle. And you're Irelynn, that woman who knows Quinty, right?"

That woman? "Yes."

Isabelle's scrutiny traveled from Irelynn's head to her toes as she gave her the once-over. She flung her long blonde hair over her shoulder. Dressed in expensive clothing with flashy jewelry, Isabelle appeared classy compared to Irelynn's drab and stained appearance. *I should have spent more time cleaning up before heading to the store.*

"Quinty's favorite food is pizza, so I'm going to make him some homemade pizza for when he comes over tonight. You did know we were dating, right?

"Really?" *That makes no sense, what with yesterday's kiss.*

"Yes. He and I were high school sweethearts. By the way, have you heard about the new house he's building? Of course, he's *always* building new houses thanks to his stellar reputation as one of the top builders in Chokecherry Heights, but have you heard about the *latest*?"

"One of the houses in the Waterbury Acres Subdivision?"

"Oh, not the ones in *that* subdivision. That's old news." Isabelle rolled her eyes. "I'm talking about the one he's building for himself. Surely, you know about *that* one?"

"I hadn't heard he was building a house for himself, but he is remodeling one he is planning to purchase on Whitmore Street."

"You poor dear. You're so out of the loop, Irelynn."

She was?

"He hasn't made it public knowledge yet—you know how secretive he can be—but he recently changed his mind."

Quinton secretive?

Isabelle toyed with a flashy bracelet, smirking the type of smirk Irelynn recalled seeing on mean girls in high school. "He took my suggestion and is going to renovate that hideous house on Whitmore Street and flip it. Real estate in Chokecherry Heights is hot right now, what with it growing like it is. Some newcomer would surely not mind living in *that* neighborhood." Isabelle's expression shifted, mimicking one of someone who had just eaten a spoiled piece of fruit. "Quinton wouldn't ever live there. He's much more high class than that. I mean, really."

What is wrong with my neighborhood?

"He said it was his intent to remodel it and live in it himself." Quinton had seemed so excited about his house. He'd have no reason to lie to her, would he? Quinton had made it clear he cared first and foremost about the twins, and she remembered him mentioning building would take too long.

"Puhleeze. That's what he's telling everyone, but it's not exactly true. Quinty would so not live there. He only chose to purchase it because it's been on the market literally forever, and I was able to secure an incredible sales price for him." She puffed up and straightened her already super-straight posture. "The house he's building for himself is in the new subdivision on Quarter Horse Lane. He even asked me what color of walls I thought would work for the living room. It's touching how much he values my opinion."

"Oh." What else could she say? Quinton hadn't mentioned this to her.

"But you wouldn't know anything about that. Anyway, I am thrilled he cares so much about my choices for wall color. He's even mentioned installing a swimming pool since I love to swim. But what can I say? Quinty is hot-looking and owns his own business. What's there not to like?" Another sharp smirk. "I think I've found myself the perfect catch."

Irelynn had no idea how to respond.

Max leaned over and dropped a box of crackers from the cart. Mia started pumping her legs back and forth. "Can we go?"

"I won't keep you, as I see your children need discipline. Chow for now."

Chow for now?

Isabelle sauntered off in her high heels and tight skinny jeans, leaving Irelynn with a headache from the real estate agent's obnoxious perfume. Max continued to unload the cart, and if she didn't pay attention, the eggs would be next. Mia kept asking over and over if they could go now.

"Yes, we'll go. Max, please leave the things in the cart or there'll be no cookies for you."

Irelynn retrieved the items and placed them back in the cart. Two more items and she could leave this store and pretend she'd never run into the snotty Isabelle.

Except she had. And Isabelle mentioned she and Quinton were dating. What about yesterday's kiss? The closeness that had transpired between them in recent days? The embraces? Had Irelynn imagined it all?

Didn't Quinton have feelings for her? It had seemed as though he did.

Why would Quinton kiss her if he was dating someone else? Why, if he and Isabelle were dating, wasn't Isabelle concerned about the time Irelynn and Quinton were spending together, or did she know?

She shoved aside the impulse to jump to a conclusion.

Asking Quinton was the best course of action.

A horrible thought occurred to her: could Irelynn really survive sharing custody of the kids if he married that mean-spirited woman?

No, if there was one thing she learned through the entire "sole custody" ordeal, it was that, as tempting as it may be, she would not believe something until she'd had a chance to speak with Quinton about it. There may have been a misunderstanding on the house, but given what she knew about Quinton's character, he wouldn't lie to her.

If anyone was lying, it was Isabelle.

"PLEASE CAN we make Uncle Quinton some cookies?" Mia begged.

"Pease?" asked Max. "I was good in the car."

Yes, but not at the store.

The wall clock indicated it was almost too late to start cookies.

Her mind reverted back to Quinton. What reason would he have for deceiving her? They were getting along so well. She had feelings for him and thought the feelings were mutual.

No, she wouldn't believe Isabelle. The more she got to know Quinton, the more she respected his upstanding character.

Irelynn continued the war with herself and, in the end, the cookies won.

QUINTON TEXTED IRELYNN, asking her to meet him at his new house so they could for a run after he met with the concrete guy. He couldn't wait to see her again, even though it had been only yesterday. He recalled how she felt in his arms and how his lips felt on hers. What would it be like to kiss her fully again and for longer?

He strode around the house, mentally checking off the things needing to be done outdoors. It was a minor miracle the home had passed inspection with only a few minor hiccups, which the owner's son would have to fix before the closing date, namely bringing the electrical wiring up to code. Thankfully, there had been no water damage; no radon leaks; the fireplace, chimney, and plumbing passed scrutiny; and the HVAC system had been installed fairly recently and was fully functioning. Quinton had negotiated a lower price due to the extensive cleaning and cosmetic repairs the home required. All new flooring, paint, and windows would lend to bringing the home as close to new as possible. He also intended to replace the fence in the backyard and plant fresh sod.

In short, the renovation would take time and would cost him plenty, but hard work, frugality, and determination were on his side.

The possibilities of what this home—his home—could be permeated his thoughts. The transformation when he completed all he wanted to do would have impressed Dad. Quinton could add things, like a home office, later. Irelynn would probably really appreciate a home office for her website building projects.

Wait a minute, Gregory. You're getting ahead of yourself. If he was adding a home office for Irelynn, that would mean...*yeah, way ahead of yourself. Remember, you're not marriage material.*

But maybe he was after all.

He and Irelynn would make a phenomenal team raising the twins. Gram would be thrilled, and it would be what Nicole wanted.

Except that Quinton knew this was no longer for Nicole. His feelings for Irelynn were real. Plain and simple.

Quinton finished speaking with the concrete guy about what

it would take to fix the huge crack in the driveway and waited for Irelynn to arrive.

Sure enough, a few minutes later, she arrived, twins in tow. He was really looking forward to a run. With her.

"Hey, Irelynn."

"Hi, Quinton."

"Hey, Mia and Max. Ready to go to the playground?"

"Yes, we made you cookies." Mia handed him a plate of chocolate chip cookies.

"Then I guess I should have one before we go." He took a bite and let the chocolate chips melt in his mouth. "These are delicious. Thank you."

"And thank you again for putting in the mailbox and the post. I didn't see the charges for those or the area rugs on the statement."

"It's all taken care of."

Irelynn nodded. "Thank you. I really appreciate that."

"No problem." He took another bite.

"Quinton? Can we talk for a minute before we go?"

"Sure. What's up?"

Concern filled her eyes. "I saw Isabelle at Shifflett's yesterday."

"Oh, really?"

"Yes, she said something I need to clarify with you."

Quinton would have rather started the day off *not* talking about Isabelle, but since it was important to Irelynn, and he wanted to fix whatever was bothering her, he encouraged her to continue.

"Isabelle mentioned you are building a house for yourself in that new Quarter Horse Lane subdivision and that you wouldn't be living here."

"She did, did she? Where did Isabelle come up with that?" Figured Isabelle would fabricate a story to endanger his budding relationship with Irelynn. The realization frustrated him.

Irelynn shrugged. "I have no idea. It didn't make sense, since you voiced your desire to purchase and renovate this house to live in with Mia and Max."

"And I still plan to do that. I couldn't afford to build a house for myself in that subdivision. They're talking strict covenants and considerable square footages."

"Can we have more snacks?" Mia asked.

"More snacks for Max," Max added.

Irelynn kneeled in front of the stroller. "I don't have any more snacks, but we'll go to the playground in just a few minutes."

"Pwayground," nodded Max. He sat back in his seat, a grin on his round face.

Irelynn stood again and faced Quinton. "I know it's not my business about your personal life, but she did also mention the two of you were dating."

Quinton frowned. "No, we're not dating."

"Something about being high school sweethearts."

"What? No. I have never liked Isabelle that way. We attended a school where everyone knew everyone else. Naturally, most students got along with each other. Isabelle had a reputation for mastering the art of making others feel inferior, especially since her family is one of the wealthiest in Chokecherry Heights."

"I doubted her story, but she was pretty convincing."

Quinton should have known Isabelle would attempt something like this. He twisted his neck from one side to the other, eliciting a much-needed pop from the tense muscles. "There are a few things you should know about Isabelle. She can be volatile and devious. In hindsight, I see I made a huge mistake in not setting her straight in the beginning about our supposed relationship. I guess I feared jeopardizing the sale of the home."

~

IRELYNN HAD no reason to believe Quinton wasn't being upfront with her. Isabelle's condescending personality was on par with what he mentioned about her in high school.

He took a step toward her. "I'm sorry, Irelynn, that I didn't set her straight. I'd like to think I don't procrastinate, but I guess I do on some things. She likes to flirt and I should have nipped that in the bud right away, whether she found a way to manipulate the sale or not."

"I just wanted to make sure where I stood with you." If he had been romantically interested in Irelynn while dating Isabelle, Irelynn would have been devastated. Memories revisited of Mom sobbing in her bedroom that night after finding out Dad had a girlfriend. It had started the worst fight ever between them. The fight that caused Dad to leave and never return.

Irelynn would not be like Mom in that way. She'd not allow a man to hurt her the way Dad had hurt Mom.

"Where you stand with me?" Quinton put a hand on his chin. "I can tell you two things. Number one, Isabelle and I are not dating. Number two, I do have a crush on someone."

"Really? Do I know her?" The teasing in his eyes told her where this was going.

"You might. Let's see, she's smart, witty, gorgeous, is about 5′6″, and is slender with stunning green eyes and long brown hair. She's athletic, a loving mom, and she has a penchant for running, pizza, coffee, and air hockey. Do you know her?"

"She sounds familiar."

Quinton cupped her face in his hands. "I have a crush on you, Irelynn Brady."

"What's a crush?" Mia asked, interrupting the moment.

Irelynn and Quinton both laughed at her inquisition.

"Hello?" Two people from the neighboring home strolled toward them. A tall elderly woman with a fashionable gray bob, plaid pants, and a string of pearls around the collar of her lime green blouse introduced herself as Mrs. Potter. "And this is my husband, Mr. Potter," she said, pointing at the man at her side who was several inches shorter and rounder than his wife. He sported denim man capris that reached between his knees and ankles and a white t-shirt with the lettering, "World's Most Awesome Grandpa."

"I'm Irelynn, this is Quinton, and this is Mia and Max."

"Pleasure to meet you all," said Mrs. Potter. "Pardon my excessive curiosity, but are you, by chance, the young family who will make this..." she paused and gestured in the house's direction, "this place a soon-to-be appealing home?"

Mr. Potter cocked his head in their direction, a hearing aid visible behind his thinning hair. "Could be real a real nice place if someone had the fortitude to fix it up."

"That's what we aim to do," said Quinton. His face shone with pride, and Irelynn knew if anyone succeeded in rehabbing the run-down property, it would be him.

Mrs. Potter leaned her head toward the stroller. "What adorable children. Say, would you two like to do me a favor? If it's all right with your mother, of course." She eyed Irelynn, and continued. "Do you see all of those elegant yellow flowers in my yard? How about you all go pick them for me for a bouquet for my dining room table?"

Irelynn's heart warmed at Mrs. Potter's words indicating her relationship to the twins. "Can we go pick yellow flowers?" Mia asked.

"Fwowers," copied Max.

"Yes, you may." Irelynn unhooked the seatbelt harnesses and released Mia and Max, who exuberantly leaped from their seats and did Mrs. Potter's bidding.

"Now then, such a project will keep them occupied while we finish chatting. Mr. Potter and I have six children, 20 grandchildren, and 4 great-grands, so we know all about keeping children entertained while the adults talk." She paused. "Mr. Potter, what time do you have?"

"The time I show is 2:52 p.m."

"Marvelous, we have about five minutes to chat before we have our bingo game at the senior citizen center. I am the vice-president of the Neighborhood Lookout Society. I have been vying for the presidential position, but until then, I shall be content in my role as second-in-command. Nonetheless, it is my sincere pleasure to welcome you to the neighborhood."

"It's a warm and friendly neighborhood," added Mr. Potter.

They continued their conversation until Mia and Max presented Mrs. Potter with a sizeable bouquet of dandelions and it was time for the Potters to leave.

"Oh, my, yes, Mr. Potter, are you ready? We mustn't be late for bingo." The couple took a few steps before Irelynn overheard Mrs. Potter say, "Remember when we were a young married couple?"

"That I do, Mrs. Potter. That I do."

Irelynn thought about Mrs. Potter's insinuation she and Quinton were married. It bothered her far less than it had in recent days. She strapped the twins into the stroller and asked Quinton, "Ready for our run?"

"Yes, but first..."

Quinton's warm lips met hers, and his arms wrapped around her waist. Irelynn could sense the passion, but also the tenderness in his kiss. It was everything she had hoped it would be. And more.

Her arms wrapped around his neck, and he pulled her closer. Irelynn's heart raced, as she gave in to the intensity of Quinton's kiss.

The feeling was mutual. She was in love with Quinton Gregory.

CHAPTER 26

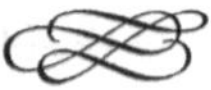

She spied the older woman from her front yard one sunny day while Mia and Max showed their artistic side with sidewalk chalk on the driveway.

Irelynn waved at her neighbor, who was sitting on her porch scribbling furiously in her notebook.

Noting the children were behaving and she needed a moment of adult conversation, she wandered over to Mrs. Caruthers. The woman promptly closed her notebook and placed the pen in the spiral.

"Do you ever share what's in the pages of your notebook?" Irelynn asked, hoping for a glimpse into the mysterious diary.

"Hardly. It's confidential information limited to being viewed by the president of the Neighborhood Lookout Society."

"Does it give details on all the neighbors?"

"Yes, no one is excluded." Mrs. Caruthers cocked her head to one side. "Are you attempting to have me divulge private information?"

"No, that's not it at all. I was just wondering if you could give me a few random details about the neighborhood."

"I did already show you my sketches of the man looking at the ramshackle home down the block."

"Yes, thank you for that."

"It's my understanding your handsome young fellow is interested in the home."

Irelynn was taken aback. "How do you know that?"

"I am the president of the Neighborhood Lookout Society. It's my business to know these things. Is he going to fix it up and sell it?"

Should she divulge to Mrs. Caruthers Quinton's plan? She decided to change the subject instead. "Do you know why the home is in such bad condition?"

Mrs. Caruthers licked a finger and flipped through a few of the pages. Irelynn leaned forward and allowed her eyes to dart across the pages, while attempting to avoid being obvious. Mrs. Caruthers's ginormous, but illegible, slanted writing filled the lines.

"Let's see. Well, I suppose I can tell you the background story."

Irelynn peered at the twins to be sure they weren't up to mischief. Mia trotted toward her, a piece of yellow sidewalk chalk in her hand. "Come see our pictures," she said, pointing to Irelynn's decorated driveway.

"I will in a few minutes, honey."

"Can we draw on Mrs. Ruthers's diveway?" Mia asked.

Mrs. Caruthers shook her head with haste. "My, but no. No fancy artwork in my yard."

"Why don't you draw a picture of us at the playground next to your other pictures?" Irelynn asked.

"Okay," Mia dashed over to Irelynn's yard once again.

"Now where were we? Oh, yes, I was about to tell you some privileged information about why the house at 1446 Whitmore Street is in such disrepair." Mrs. Caruthers cast one more peek inside her notebook, then closed it. "Back in the day, Mr. Lloyd, a bizarre elderly man, lived at the home. He was a hoarder of ginormous proportions. Everything from books, newspapers, and magazines to collectibles and old engine parts. The house actually looks better than it has in a long time."

"Did he pass away?"

"He did. And, I believe it was his son who stopped by and attempted to clean up the grounds after he inherited it. Not sure what the interior looks like. Mr. Lloyd was a slob even in his younger years, much to the disturbance of the rest of the neighborhood." She paused to inhale some much-needed oxygen. "Word on the street is, when his son came over and saw the condition of the home, he decided it would be better to sell it than to try to rehab it. Apparently, Mr. Lloyd allowed his eight dogs to take over the house and he never cleaned up after himself or his pets."

"Was he unable to care for the home due to his age?"

Mrs. Caruthers harumphed. "Hardly. For as long as I have resided on Whitmore Street, he'd never been one to take pride in home ownership. The house fell into disrepair soon after Mr. Lloyd's purchase of it and it's been an eyesore ever since."

Irelynn couldn't wait to share with Quinton that, while she hadn't been fortunate enough to see the contents of Mrs. Caruthers's notebook, she had been successful in getting her neighbor to begrudgingly reveal some of the contents within.

He'd be so envious.

AFTER NEARLY 45 LONG DAYS, closing day on the Whitmore Street house arrived and Quinton waited in the Chokecherry Heights Land and Title conference room, early for his appointment.

He ran a hand through his hair.

Offered another silent prayer for wisdom and guidance.

Finished the remaining water in the complimentary water bottle the receptionist handed him on arrival.

Tamped the excitement coursing through his wired veins.

After all this, he'd go for a run before returning to the Waterbury Acres house.

Today he would cement one of the biggest decisions in his life —to become a homeowner.

Plans for his first project for the house consumed his mind.

Isabelle stepped through the open door. "Quinty, you're here early."

"Excited to become a homeowner."

She took a seat next to him at the rectangular table. "That blue shirt really brings out the color in your eyes," she cooed.

Quinton took a deep breath and sneaked a peak at his fitness tracker. Ten minutes until the actual closing.

"I noticed the theater in the city is hosting a brand-new play next week. How about you and I go and get reacquainted? You know, catch up on all the happenings in our lives between high school and now."

"Isabelle, I appreciate our friendship."

"Yes, and it's time to take that to the next level."

He shifted in his seat. Hadn't he always prided himself in being upfront? Of tackling things head-on? Sure, he wanted this closing to go through without a snag, couldn't afford to jeopardize it, but honesty trumped all else. Especially after the lies she told Irelynn.

Isabelle leaned closer. "Such a thinking man. What's on your mind, Quinty?"

Quinton blew out a deep breath. "Isabelle, I appreciate your friendship."

"Yes, what is there not to appreciate?"

"And your assistance with the purchase of this home."

"I'd prefer you flip it rather than live in it, and I did take a monumental cut in commission due to the reduced price, but you're welcome." She fiddled with her necklace. "So, what do you say about going out for dinner this evening to celebrate the sale?"

"It's never going to be more than friendship for us, Isabelle."

She snapped her head back, her eyes narrowing. "What are you saying, Quinty?"

"It's Quinton, and I'm saying that while I think of you as a friend, it can't be any more than that."

"Is there someone else?"

Irelynn's image flashed through his mind. Going for a run to the playground, challenging him to air hockey, baking cookies with Mia, sitting side-by-side in church, kissing her..."Yes, there is."

"Don't tell me it's that dowdy woman whose opinion you wanted on the house."

"Yes, it's Irelynn."

Isabelle shook her head. "Maybe all that sawdust you expose yourself to has messed with your mind." She skidded her chair across the wood flooring, causing an obnoxious scraping noise. "You do realize I can influence whether the finalization of the sale of this decrepit house goes through, right?"

"I do realize that, and I don't want to hurt you, Isabelle, but there is no 'us' beyond friendship. I love Irelynn."

"Fine," she hissed, standing and stomping toward the open door. "I'll be back when the other party arrives."

QUINTON JOINED Gram and her friends for their weekly game of Uno that evening. "How did the closing go?" Gram asked.

"Are you a homeowner yet?" Mrs. Pierce sneakily played two cards during one turn.

Quinton inwardly chuckled. As long as they didn't get any wacky schemes in their minds about what would happen if he lost a game to them, he'd allow the octogenarians to practice some minor sleight of hand. "I am. The paperwork is signed and the mansion at 1446 Whitmore Street belongs to yours truly."

Miss Bea set her cards on the table facedown and clapped her hands. "Now that is what we like to hear."

"Proud of you," said Gram.

"Thanks."

"Now for the next plan," suggested Miss Bea, this time rubbing her hands together.

Quinton prepared himself for her next words. "What's that?"

"You can't be living in that house all by your lonesome."

Mrs. Pierce nodded, "indeed."

"Refresh my memory on the square footage," said Gram.

"It's around 2,300 square feet."

Mrs. Pierce's mouth dropped open. "That's no pint-sized abode."

"Naturally. That's what I'm getting at," said Miss Bea, sitting up straighter in her chair. "You see, no man in his right mind would want to reside in a house of that enormity all by himself. Why, it's inconceivable."

"Inconceivable and lonely." Mrs. Pierce shivered.

Quinton shook his head. He had been around Gram's crazy friends long enough to see where all this was going. "No worries, ladies. It can't be lonely with two children."

Miss Bea rolled her eyes. "You missed my hint. Yes, I know you have two children now and they will fill the rooms with laughter and joy, but there's something missing."

"A wife. You need a wife in that house," said Mrs. Pierce.

"And we know just the one," added Gram.

Somehow, their conniving plot about his matrimonial future failed to bother him as much as it once had.

CHAPTER 27

Today was Nicole's birthday. If she had lived, she would be 26 years old. Irelynn fought the tears as she emerged from her car. While Mom had the twins, she figured she would stop by Nicole's grave site and "visit" with her friend for a few minutes.

Not that Nicole was still there. No, Irelynn knew her best friend was in the presence of her loving Savior rather than in the coffin in which she was buried, but that didn't make it any easier for the ones Nicole left behind.

Irelynn shut the car door and began the short walk to Nicole's humble grave marker. The birds chirped, the air smelled of pending summer, and all would be right with the world.

If only Nicole had survived.

As she came up over the slight hill to the area where Nicole was buried, Irelynn saw someone else sitting at the gravesite. Knees pulled to his chest. Head low.

Quinton.

She took a step closer. She shouldn't interrupt this special time between brother and sister, but something drew her closer. Irelynn willed her steps to be light.

"I can't seem to forgive myself for that day, Nicole." Quinton's voice was raw and filled with emotion.

Forgive himself for what?

Irelynn really should retreat and head over to Mom's to retrieve the twins. She could "visit" Nicole another time.

But instead, she kept walking toward her friend's gravesite.

"I hope you can forgive me someday. Of course, I know you're not here, but just talking to you this way brings me comfort." Quinton cleared his throat. "If I had moved quicker, reacted faster when I sensed the danger, I know Tom would still be here. The bombs and explosions and gunshots were everywhere. If I had planned better..." Quinton's voice drifted.

He blamed himself for Tom's death?

Irelynn had heard Tom had been killed when insurgents bombed the area he was in, but she'd never heard the entire story. Maybe Nicole hadn't either. Quinton confirmed her thoughts with his next words.

"I didn't want to tell you all this back then, Nicole. You were struggling to raise two children, and with Mom and Dad having died just a couple years earlier. It was all too much. But you have to know I beat myself up every day wondering what I could have done differently to save Tom. I know you loved him so much." Thick emotion laced Quinton's words.

Guilt permeated through Irelynn. She really shouldn't be listening to this private conversation. But yet, her feet wouldn't budge. She was so close now she could take three or four more steps and reach out to him if she chose.

Her heart was his now. It wouldn't be out of the realm of possibility to render comfort to him.

"Can you forgive me, sis? Forgive me for not saving Tom? For not acting faster when I sensed the threat was there? Not keeping my promise to you to bring Tom home? I know I promised—and I wanted to keep that promise more than anything I've ever wanted in my whole life." He took a deep breath. Tears misted

Irelynn's eyes. "Disappointing you when I made that promise is something I never wanted to do. Now the kids don't have a mom or a dad. They're stuck with Irelynn and me."

Quinton shifted, and Irelynn feared he would see her there. She really must go, but the temptation to stay won.

"It's rough here without you and without Mom and Dad and without Tom. Yes, there's Gram and there's the twins, but the three of us need everyone here. I'm not sure why God allowed all this, only that He did." Quinton sighed. "I want to keep the promise I made to you all those months ago while you lay in your hospital bed with the cancer. The promise to raise Mia and Max and take care of them and love them the way you and Tom would have. But it's tough, Nicole. I don't want to fail at that too."

His voice cracked, and Irelynn knew he was close to crying. She attempted to stifle the sobs rising within her throat.

Something about Quinton's vulnerable position at the gravesite made her want to reach out to him. Hold him. Comfort him. Mourn Nicole's death together. Mourn broken promises and high expectations and failures and...

But she couldn't just walk up and wrap her arms around him. Not that it would be such a bad thing. When people cared about each other, they consoled each other.

Irelynn closed her eyes and prayed for Quinton instead. Prayed he would be able to release this guilt he felt pressed upon himself. She opened her eyes again and stared at his back. She still had time to leave. She could come back later.

"So anyway, happy birthday, Nicole. I hold on to the memories of when we were kids doing crazy stunts to keep Mom and Dad on their toes, the times we told people we were identical twins, and then gave them an odd look when they just didn't see it." He paused and gave a low, sad chuckle. "And those days as teens when we went camping and fishing with Mom and Dad. I want to promise I'll revive the memories of the camping trips and build a treehouse with the twins, but I'm afraid to make those promises. Afraid I'll fail again."

Irelynn sniffled then, realizing too late that Quinton could and would hear her. And he did.

Quinton turned to face her, anger in his eyes. "What are you doing here?"

"I'm sorry, Quinton, I was coming to tell Nicole happy birthday. I didn't know you were going to be here too."

"How long have you been standing there?"

Irelynn was tempted to say "not long," but she knew that would be an out-and-out lie. She glanced at her fitness tracker. "Ten minutes, maybe? But I didn't see your truck parked anywhere. I didn't see you until I got closer." The excuses sounded lame in her ears.

He stood, hands balled at his side. Hurt flashing across his face. "What did you hear?"

"Quinton..."

"No, Irelynn, what did you hear?"

"I heard you apologize to Nicole and the stuff about Tom." She reached up and swished a tear away with the back of her hand.

"That wasn't for you to hear."

"I hadn't intended to."

"It was private." His voice rose. "Private between Nicole and me. You had no right."

"Quinton, I didn't intend to come here and invade your privacy. I came here wanting to talk to Nicole. I know she's not here anymore, but it gives me comfort to visit her on occasion. Just like it does you. I had no idea you were here."

"And you couldn't have turned around and walked back to your car? Out of respect?"

"I should have. I regret that now."

"Yeah, you should have." He stomped past her, his footsteps

loud on the sidewalk leading to the gravesite. Quinton continued on and didn't stop until he was out of her view.

Regret tugged at Irelynn's heart in such a powerful way she wasn't sure she'd ever forgive herself.

~

HE HEARD her call to him. But he didn't stop. Instead, Quinton took huge strides, almost breaking into a run to get to his truck and drive away.

He and Irelynn had grown closer in recent weeks. Things were going well. But this complicated matters.

Quinton sprinted, his feet hitting the sidewalk. He wished he hadn't parked so far away, as he rounded the opposite edge of the cemetery.

Irelynn had no right to listen in on his conversation. It was private, just between him and Nicole.

And not only did she have no right to listen in on his conversation, she had no right to *continue* listening. Irelynn should have respected his privacy. Why hadn't she?

Anger mixed with frustration filled his entire being. How could he face her again when she knew the truth about his broken promise to Nicole, his failure to keep Tom safe, and return him home to his family?

Now she knows the "real" you.

It was probably prideful, but Quinton didn't want anyone outside of Gram, the pastor, and his therapist to know the "true" him.

Especially not Irelynn.

He became a pro at retreating beneath his façade. The military hero. The doting uncle. The Godly man whose faith was important to him. The owner of his own growing business. Successfully dealing with the deaths of his parents and his sister in a span of a few years. Successfully caring for two young kids. A new homeowner. Not a problem in the world.

Yet, Irelynn had heard him reveal the truth. He wasn't the man who had it all together as he claimed.

Quinton climbed into his truck and sped away. He needed to get back to the jobsite, but he needed some time to sort things out first.

Lord, please help me with this. He knew not what to specifically pray, but Quinton did know he had an Intercessor who would bring his pleas to the Lord.

IRELYNN HADN'T SEEN Quinton in two days. She attempted to call and text him, but the calls went to voicemail, and the texts went unanswered. She regretted listening to his time with Nicole. Would he forgive her?

She had relished the whirlwind of time spent together. She had grown fond of the man she once considered her nemesis. She laughed to herself when she thought of his progression from a somewhat-of-a-nemesis, to a sort-of-a-nemesis, to a bit-of-a-nemesis, to a not-really-a nemesis; and finally, to not-a-nemesis at all.

They complimented each other. Sat by each other in church now, on purpose, spent time talking on the porch under Mrs. Caruthers's strict scrutiny, and had discussed ways to help the twins deal with the lingering pain of losing their mom.

But now Irelynn had blown the whole thing.

She prayed God would assist her in making amends. Her reliance on Him had become even more profound in these past months of caring for the children. He'd come through for her on mothering, the job issue, and so much more. Surely the Good Lord would assist her with this issue as well.

When Quinton arrived to retrieve the twins, he avoided her eye.

"Quinton." She reached for his arm. "We need to talk."

"I need to go. I'm taking the twins to see Gram."

"Please. Just a few minutes."

The tortured look in his blue eyes crushed her.

"Please." She took his hand and led him to the couch. "Mia and Max, can you go build Uncle Quinton a creation with your building blocks while you wait?"

"Is he okay?" Mia asked, her blonde brows knitted together in concern.

"I'm fine, Mia. We'll leave in a few minutes, all right?"

Mia and Max raced off, leaving Irelynn and Quinton alone on the couch. "Quinton, will you please forgive me? I'm sorry I listened in."

"It was a private conversation."

"I know that."

"Then why did you stay?"

The accusation in his voice nearly undid her. She cared for him. More than she ought. Was falling for him—hard. Now, with his narrowed eyes and standoffish demeanor, Irelynn wasn't sure what to do.

Lord, please give me the words. Heal this situation.

"I...," she paused. "I don't know why I did. But, Quinton, I know you miss Nicole. I miss her too."

"But you didn't fail her."

"I felt like I almost did."

Quinton studied her. "How do you mean?"

She took a deep breath. There was a time when she dared not reveal her insecurities about raising the twins for fear he might not think her capable. But now? Now she just needed to remedy the current situation. All pride aside. "I was so scared I wouldn't be able to support Mia and Max. I struggle with finances, and with the remodel and my job being cut to part time, I just wasn't sure. That and I had never been a mom before."

"I didn't realize you were struggling with your finances. You should have said something."

"I couldn't say something and risk you thinking Nicole made a mistake in asking me to co-raise them. Following her wishes and keeping my promise to her is so important. I understand that it is for you too, Quinton."

He stretched his neck from one side to the other, causing a loud cracking noise. "Look, Irelynn. You really don't understand. I let her down because I let her husband die. After I promised to bring him back alive."

Irelynn's heart lurched. She'd heard him blame himself at Nicole's gravesite, but to hear it again broke her heart. She leaned forward and took his face in her hands. "There is no way I believe that."

Quinton cleared his throat, but he didn't attempt to move. "I promised her, but when the insurgents came in and I dragged two guys out of there, one lived. One didn't. The one that didn't was Tom."

"I'm so sorry." She knew not what else to say.

"I tried my best, but..."

"I don't know why the Lord chose to take Nicole, and I don't understand why he took Tom too. But, Quinton, you did your best. You risked your life to save him and the other soldier. You have to believe you did all you could."

Silence ensued and Irelynn scoured the rooms from her vantage point on the couch. The twins seemed to be enthralled with their building project. She removed her hands from Quinton's face and reached for his hand. "*I know* you did what you could. If Nicole were here, she would know you did what you could."

"How do you know that?"

She tightened her hand on his, and he didn't resist. "Because I know the kind of man you are. You're a hero. You would do all you could to save your brother-in-law. For some reason, it wasn't God's plan that he would survive, and I don't know why."

"I didn't want you to know."

"Why?"

"Because I was afraid you'd think less of me."

How could she ever think less of him? Not now that she really was beginning to know him. "Quinton, I don't think less of you."

"I attend a PTSD therapy group and see a therapist and the pastor for counseling. I have since leaving active duty. I'm not the guy who has it all together like people think I am."

"So you're broken? So am I. That's why we need Jesus. We cling to Him when we struggle through things like this. Me with trying to mother the kids and financial difficulties and struggling at times to realize that God does love and care for me, even though my earthly father never did. But He does care. He is there for us. He does heal us. His Word says so."

Quinton released her hand and put his arm around her. "Thank you."

"For?"

"For caring enough to sort this whole mess out. I'm sorry I was so brash about it."

"You forgive me, then?"

"Yes."

"Thank you. Look, Quinton, we have the twins to raise. We are going to do this as a team, just like Nicole wanted. We'll succeed in raising them to know the Lord, and hopefully to become productive, kind, and caring adults. We can do this with His help. And I'm proud of you for seeking help with the pain from fighting in Afghanistan."

His lips found hers then. Passionate, yet tender. Deepening as the seconds passed, and making Irelynn yearn for it not to end. His arms held her tight, and she returned his embrace.

When they finished their kiss, Quinton drew back from her. "We'll make a 'go' of this, won't we?"

"We will."

Quinton kissed her again, his lips warm on hers. She knew she could kiss this man forever if it weren't for two tiny words chorused by a tiny little-boy voice. "Ewww. Gwoss."

CHAPTER 28

Several weeks later, Quinton pulled out the chair for Irelynn, and she took a seat, inhaling the aroma of the savory and spicy food served at Fernandez's. He took his place across from her.

This date had the makings of being far better than it could ever have been the first time Nicole suggested it.

The waitress, a teen with a mouthful of braces, greeted them and placed a complimentary basket of chips and a bowl of salsa in front of them.

"The special is steak or chicken fajitas with rice and beans." She handed them each a menu. "I'll give you time to decide."

Their gazes intertwined and he grinned. Over the past several months, she had really grown to like his smile. And him.

Quinton took a chip from the basket and dipped it into the salsa. "I thought I'd never care to eat the chips and salsa from here after a certain someone stood me up for our official first date."

"That's nothing compared to what happened to me when a certain someone stood me for our official first date. I was in a carb coma for days after downing a full bread bowl at Fernando's. Finally, we get to have the date that never happened."

They laughed together then, the easy camaraderie between them apparent.

"Poor Nicole," said Irelynn, attempting to catch her breath. "She had no idea she told you the date was at Fernandez's and told me the date was at Fernando's." Irelynn never would have guessed she would one day laugh about being stood up for a date.

"She had an ornery streak, but I do know how much she wanted us to get together."

"And who names two restaurants in a small town such similar names?"

Quinton ate another chip. "To be fair, Fernandez's has been here for about 20 years. Fernando's came along just last year. It doesn't hold a candle to The Pizza Slice."

"And no air hockey either."

He chuckled. "True. Oh, I almost forgot...in honor of our real first date, I found something for us."

"Oh?"

Before he could answer, the waitress returned for their orders. After she left to tend to another customer, Quinton pulled his phone from his pocket and started to scroll. "I found some ice breaker questions for first dates."

"Icebreakers? An introvert's worst nightmare."

"And an extrovert's best dream since we always want to know all about everyone else."

Irelynn giggled. She did want to know more about him, so this would be fun.

"You ready?" Quinton asked, glancing down at his phone.

"Ready."

"All right. What's your favorite color?"

"Burgundy. Yours?"

"Blue."

Irelynn rolled her eyes. "Typical guy." Her gaze caught his and her heart thrummed in her chest. So, this was what it was like to be in love. And in love with a former nemesis, no doubt. Talk about ironies.

"So, I think we know the answer to this one," Quinton continued. "What's your limit when it comes to social interaction?"

"As an introvert, it doesn't take long for social interaction to be too much. I'd say a few minutes of idle chitchat with a stranger and I'm done for."

"A few minutes of idle chitchat is never enough."

"For an extrovert."

Quinton chuckled. "For an extrovert." He analyzed the list, as if choosing only the most interesting questions. "How about, if there was an Olympic competition for activities we do every day, what is something you'd gold medal in?"

"That's easy. Stepping on Max's toy building blocks; tripping over Mia's dolly clothing; rushing around like a crazy person trying to get enough things done before they wake up from their nap. Basically, something in the agility category. You?"

"Hmmm. Probably a gold medal for sticking my foot in my mouth or getting stuck in cramped slides."

Their laughter mingled. "Yes, you would win a medal for that one for sure."

They continued answering the questions until their food arrived. Quinton blessed their meal, and they began to eat, the atmosphere and silence relaxing and comfortable.

After several minutes, Irelynn asked how the house was coming along. She knew he had been working diligently on it. The exterior was not cleaned up and presentable, and he recently showed her a portion of the interior. Quinton possessed a knack for transforming a battered home into not only a habitable, but a homey place to live. The twins would love their new rooms.

"It's really coming along. The outside is just about finished, the painting is done on the inside, and the flooring will be installed on Wednesday. You should come see it on Thursday after the install. You won't believe it's the same place. Of course, we had a dozen loads taken to the landfill."

"Super impressive, Quinton. I would love to come see it. And I'm sure Mrs. Caruthers has documented the entire process with detailed accuracy."

"Maybe she drew more sketches with a before and after picture. If you're sneaky, you can catch another glimpse inside her notebook."

"Mrs. Caruthers might be on to me. I'm sure she's never eaten so many cookies before."

"I bet she's never been bribed by cookies before Irelynn Brady became her neighbor."

The remainder of the meal passed with warm companionship. After they finished dinner, they drove back to Irelynn's house. Mom would be ready to return home, as she had to work tomorrow.

"How did it go?" Irelynn asked Mom, as they entered the house.

Mom smiled, but had a mischievous glint in her eyes. "We had a lot of fun. They're already in bed. I think the Playdough creations we made wore them out."

Irelynn gave Mom a hug. "Thank you for taking care of them for us."

"My pleasure. Did you two have fun?"

"The food and the company were both first-rate," Quinton said, offering up his best British accent.

"Good to hear," laughed Mom. "Well, I better go." She reached for her purse, but Irelynn noticed Mom still wore a suspicious expression.

"Mom, is there something I should know?"

"What?" Mom feigned innocence with a swoop of her hand to her chest.

"Mrs. Brady, even I can see you look like a cat that ate a

canary," interjected Quinton, casually placing his arm around Irelynn.

A gesture Irelynn could easily become accustomed to with no prodding necessary.

"All right. You two are quite observant. Mr. Wilson called and asked me out to dinner."

Irelynn's mouth fell open. "Mr. Wilson, as in the Mr. Wilson at church who finds it necessary to constantly strike up a conversation with you?"

"He would be the one."

"Mom, really?"

"Is there something wrong with Mr. Wilson?"

Quinton tugged Irelynn closer to him. "Did you say 'yes'?"

"Oh, I definitely did."

"You never told me you had a crush on Mr. Wilson."

"He does seem like a nice man. So anyway, tomorrow night at Fernando's." Mom blushed, something Irelynn hadn't seen in years, if ever. A strange feeling came over her. While she was happy for Mom, she wanted nothing to hurt the woman who was so dear to her.

"As opposed to Fernandez's?" teased Quinton.

"Yes, Mom, please be sure it's the right place."

"Oh, it's Fernando's. Mr. Wilson's mom is Italian, so he loves Italian food, and as you know, I'm quite fond of it myself." Mom reached for the door. "I'd better go. I'll let you know how the date goes Sunday morning at church."

"Mom, please be sure he treats you like a gentleman and takes you home at a reasonable time, and..."

"Yes, I'll make it home by curfew. Now you and Quinton enjoy the rest of your evening."

With a final wave goodbye, Mom left the house, a radiant smile lighting her face.

～

AFTER IRELYNN'S MOM LEFT, they checked on the twins snuggled in their new rooms, then went to sit on the porch. One of the things Quinton hoped to install at his own home was a porch swing. He figured he would enjoy sitting in the cool evenings with her on the porch.

His opinion of her sure had changed in recent months.

Things were going better for sure. The twins were adjusting and having less nightmares, work was still steady, and his new house was coming along better than he ever would have expected. His PTSD steadily improved, and the guilt over Tom's death was slowly lessening. Not completely gone by any stretch, but a definite improvement.

Quinton's feelings for Irelynn had changed in a major way. Now he found himself wanting to spend the rest of his life with her.

A family with the woman he was beginning to love.

Quinton squeezed Irelynn's hand. Sitting on the porch steps had become the new normal for them after the kids were in bed. He wouldn't trade those moments alone with her.

Irelynn rested her head on his shoulder. As if it had always belonged there, nestled against him. He placed a kiss on her forehead.

"What's on your mind?" he asked.

"Mom."

"Worried about her and Mr. Wilson?"

Irelynn laughed. "How did you guess? But yes, I really hope he's not some kind of crazy lunatic or something. We hardly know him."

"Protective of your mom, are we?" he grinned, knowing he'd be the same way.

"You might say that." Irelynn sighed. When she decides to fall in love with someone, I want...I guess I want him to be worthy of her."

Quinton stroked his thumb over Irelynn's hand, hoping the gesture comforted her. "Your mom is a nice lady, and I can understand your concern. But just because Mr. Wilson asked her out doesn't mean they'll get married."

"I know, but I can tell he really likes her just from watching them interact at church."

"Yeah, and I think the feeling is mutual."

"Especially the way she blushed when she told us he asked her out. Like a teenager or something."

Quinton chuckled. "Ahhh, young love."

Irelynn joined in with his laughter. "Young love? Well, maybe not so young, but do you know anything about Mr. Wilson?"

"I know he's a teacher at the Christian school here in town and that he's gone to our church for as long as I can remember. Gram would know everything there is to know about him if you want to conduct a full background check."

"Or Mrs. Caruthers. She probably has some useful information tucked inside that notebook of hers."

"She likely knew him as a child."

"A biography neatly handwritten in a purple notebook."

Quinton squeezed her hand. "Your mom will be all right, Irelynn."

"Thanks. I just worry, you know? It's always just been the two of us."

"That protectiveness...I like that about you."

Before she could respond, Quinton claimed her lips with his. He'd wanted to kiss her the second he'd arrived to take her to Fernandez's. Then again at Fernandez's, then in the truck on the way home.

He'd make good on the time he had to wait.

"I enjoyed our date."

"I did too."

They stood, then, and Quinton wrapped his arms around her waist, and her arms found his neck.

He kissed her again. "Here's to many more dates in our future."

One Year Later

Waves crashed against the rocks, spraying up fountains of water. The sound of children splashing in the ocean waters, birds flying overhead, and a boat in the distance created the perfect scene for a honeymoon.

And two newlyweds walking along the white beaches of Maui hand-in-hand.

"What a wonderful gift Gram gave us to fly us here for a honeymoon and for Mom to watch the twins for us," Irelynn said, relishing the togetherness with her new husband.

"She thought it would be the perfect gift, and she was right. Gram said when she and Gramps got married, they couldn't afford a honeymoon farther than the next town, so when they celebrated their milestone fiftieth wedding anniversary, they flew to Maui, and stayed for two weeks. I think Gram would have stayed for a year if it weren't that Gramps liked the four seasons of Chokecherry Heights."

Quinton chuckled, and Irelynn snuggled closer and inhaled

the scent of his aftershave mixed with the salty air. Could life get any better?

"How about a run tomorrow morning on the beach?" she asked.

"That sounds inviting, and let's defeat the purpose by splitting a large pizza for lunch."

"And stopping by that retro arcade we saw in Lahaina to play some air hockey." She paused and looked up into Quinton's eyes. "I suppose I could allow you to win one game since it's our honeymoon."

"What? No, I fully intend to win *all* of the air hockey games."

"That's right. I may not have a chance against 'The Quinton,' since no one, and I mean no one, wins against 'The Quinton.' Well, except 'The Irelynn' that is."

"It's a date, but I still plan to win." Quinton drew her closer. What had made her ever think she didn't like this man? She wouldn't have wanted to miss out on him. Nicole had been right all along that they would make a great pair.

Irelynn was just too busy seeing him as a nemesis.

They admired the expansive ocean, just holding each other in the sunshine and amazing beauty of God's creation.

Finally, Quinton withdrew something from his shorts pocket. "I've been meaning to show you this before it got wet next time we decided to take a swim."

"Now you have piqued my curiosity. What is it?"

Quinton unfolded the piece of paper with a sketch on it. "This will be the new office I'm building in the basement of our house."

"*Our house*. I like the sound of that." She didn't even mind they were selling her house. Next week, they would all be moving into Quinton's newly-renovated home.

"I was thinking. We have the living room down here, which I'm sure will be filled with toys by two certain individuals." He winked at her. "That won't be a problem because they'll need to stay preoccupied while I work on the right-hand side of the home office where Gregory Home Building and Remodeling will have their office equipment set up." He paused. "And you work in your new office on the left-hand side as the owner of *Irelynn's Web Design*. I'm even having a sign made for the wall."

"Quinton, really?"

"Yes, really. You have talent, Irelynn."

His words touched her heart. "Thank you, Quinton. I can't wait."

"Glad you're excited, but just a warning, if you happen to wander over to the Gregory Home Building and Remodeling side of the office, you will have to pay some dues."

"Some dues?"

"Yep. Every time you cross the line, that's a dozen kisses."

"That's easy. You're a kissable guy."

"Am I?" He ran his fingers through her hair. "That's good then, I guess."

"Yes, and that's not even a punishment in the least. I thought you were going to say I'd have to pay in cookies or something."

"Well, that too."

They laughed together, their voices meshing with the sounds of the ocean. They dug their feet deeper into the sand and Irelynn watched as the water poured over their feet, then receded back into the ocean. Had anyone asked her if she thought she'd ever like, let alone marry Quinton Gregory a year and half ago, she would have said "no."

But God had other plans. Better plans.

"Oh, speaking of cookies," said Quinton, "and my lifetime supply..."

"Lifetime supply? Where in the marriage contract did it say anything about that?" She winked at her new husband.

"I'm sure you won't mind making a lifetime supply when you see the new oven some store in town just happened to deliver to our new kitchen."

"Quinton, really?"

"Really. Now you and Mia can bake all the cookies you want."

His lips were within inches of hers again. "I can't get enough kisses for some reason, Mrs. Gregory," he said, his voice low and husky.

"Have all the kisses you'd like, Mr. Gregory."

"You know, there's no one I'd rather have on my team of raising the twins."

"Me either."

Quinton brushed her lips with his. "Let's seal that deal then, shall we?"

And seal it, they did, as they began their new lives together.

ACKNOWLEDGMENTS

A huge thank you to my daughters. I could not have done this without you. Thank you for reading my chapters (multiple times!), for helping me brainstorm, for "holding down the fort" during the writing and polishing of this book, and for your willingness to walk alongside me in this crazy writing life—it means more to me than you will ever know. I am grateful that the Lord chose me to be your mom. What a blessing you both are to me!

To my husband, Lon. Thank you for always being willing to provide technical support for this girl who has absolutely no technical or mechanical ability. Thank you also for seeing my dream of becoming a writer as something that was possible—and urging me toward that possibility. I love you.

To my readers. May God bless and guide you as you grow in your walk with Him.

And, most importantly, thank you to my Lord and Savior, Jesus Christ. It is my deepest desire to glorify You with my writing and help bring others to a knowledge of Your saving grace.

Let the words of my mouth and the meditation of my heart be acceptable in your sight, O Lord, my rock and my redeemer. - Psalm 19:14

ABOUT THE AUTHOR

Penny Zeller is known for her heartfelt stories of faith and her passion to impact lives for Christ through fiction. While she has had a love for writing since childhood, she began her adult writing career penning articles for national and regional publications on a wide variety of topics. Today Penny is a multi-published author of several inspirational books. She is also a homeschool mom and a fitness instructor.

When Penny is not dreaming up new characters, she enjoys spending time with her husband and two daughters while camping, hiking, canoeing, reading, running, cycling, gardening, and playing volleyball.

She is represented by Tamela Hancock Murray of the Steve Laube Agency and loves to hear from her readers at her www.pennyzeller.com and her blog, *random thoughts from a day in the life of a wife, mom, and author,* at www.pennyzeller.wordpress.com.

www.ingramcontent.com/pod-product-compliance
Lightning Source LLC
Chambersburg PA
CBHW020135120726
47903CB00007B/2268